HIT DIFFERENT!

♪ ✷ #HitDifferentLife

HIT DIFFERENT!

WHEN LIFE AIN'T LIFE-ING THE WAY YOU THOUGHT, AND IT FEELS A WAY!

Written by: Denise J Lynn
Publisher: Logos Living
1st Edition

All rights reserved. No part of this book may be produced in any form without permission in writing from the author. Reviewers may quote brief passages in reviews.

Disclaimer: No part of this publication may be produced or transmitted in any form or by any means, mechanical or electronic, including photocopying or recording, or by any information storage and retrieval system, or transmitted by email without permission in writing from the publisher

Prologue	6
CHAPTER ONE	8
CHAPTER TWO	19
CHAPTER THREE	36
CHAPTER FOUR	54
CHAPTER FIVE	71
CHAPTER SIX	85
CHAPTER SEVEN	100
CHAPTER EIGHT	109
CHAPTER NINE	123
CHAPTER TEN	139
Epilogue	154

"In these streets, life's got its own playlist – full of unexpected beats and crazy remixes. When it hits different, crank up the volume and dance to the rhythm of the unknown." 🎵 💥 #HitDifferentLife

Prologue

It's that restaurant or the club that your favorite kickback that leaves you saying to yourself, "That was hittin'!". We all know there are also times when the same places and things that used to be hittin' aren't the same. Something about them just hits different. Life is crazy like that sometimes, and not what it appears to be. But think about this: hit different doesn't always mean it's a good thing. Then and there, when life swerves off your expectations, it's like a gut punch you never saw coming. But you know what? It's those crazy curveballs that make life in this sometimes ghetto earth so wild and absolutely unmissable.

Imagine the skyline, out in them streets you love so much, where skyscrapers almost touch the heavens, casting shadows that swallow up the bustling streets below. That's where our tales go down, in the back alleys and secret corners where the city's heartbeat pumps the hardest.

Amidst the wailing sirens and street vendors hustling their goods, the characters in "Hit Different" come alive. They're the dream-chasers, the ones on the grind, and the survivors against all odds. Every story in this mix gives you a sneak peek into the lives of normal people, an intimate look at their battles, and proof of how resilient and durable people can be.

But here's the flip side.

Life has this sneaky way of smacking you when you least expect it. Just when these characters think they've got it all figured out, life throws them a curveball they couldn't have seen coming if they tried. It's in those moments, those sudden twists in the plot, that "Hit Different" really shows its true colors.

These ain't your run of the mill urban tales, friend. These stories hit different, and they'll make you question some of the things you have gone through, what you are going through, and when life may be about to finesse you.

So, as we roll through the maze of "Hit Different," strap in for some surprises, for the jaw-dropping unexpected. Get ready to feel the rush, the heartbreak, and the pure adrenaline of life's insane rollercoaster. Because in this collection, life ain't life-ing the way you thought, and it sure as hell feels a way. Welcome to the world where life don't play, and it's crazy.

CHAPTER ONE

It Hit Different When You Didn't Ask For It!

The second Pastor Morrison said "Hit Different" Trina's mind immediately went to what had happened last week. She then said under her breath, "Everything hits different when you didn't ask for it"!

Katrina Thomas was a successful realtor in the Atlanta Georgia, area. Her name was Katrina, but nobody called her that. Citywide, she was known as Trina. Even more so by her business Insta handle, "Trina The Home Hottie." She was proud of her image and her success as an Influencer. It didn't hurt that she was a conventionally beautiful southern girl and shapely in all the right places.

Most wouldn't guess by looking at her, but Trina was a lady. She had a long-time boyfriend, and in everything she did, she kept it classy. But that didn't stop her from occasionally feeling the pull of danger and adventure. She had always been drawn to the wild, unpredictable side of life ever since she was a little girl, sneaking out of her bedroom window to explore the woods behind her house. And lately, that pull had been growing stronger. Until now, Trina would just go somewhere exotic for a vacation. Sometimes, she even left spontaneously, not telling anyone she was leaving.

Last week, she felt that pull again but told herself she wouldn't take it too far. Trina decided to do a staycation and visit an Airbnb out in Stone Mountain. Trina arrived at her destination, an old Victorian house perched precariously on a hill. She had booked it for a week to just wander down and take some time to relax and reflect. The community Where the house was had a real resort feel. There was a beautiful walkway that led to a man-made beach and lake. Trina went there on the first evening of her staycation. The place where the walkway met the lake was breathtaking and surreal.

The lake's surface was so clear and smooth that it was like the lake was a sheet of glass. The sun was beginning to set and reflected an orange glow on the lake's surface. Trina could see the bottom of the lake. There were rocks and dead leaves at the bottom, and they stood out against the reflection of the orange sky.

There, In front of the place where the path and the lake met, she met a glamorous older woman who said her name was Ruth. Ruth looked at Trina and said, "I never feel more alive than when I am here." Trina smiled and said, "It is beautiful here". Ruth said.

"That's not what I mean. It is beautiful here, But this lake and this place make me feel alive! Even in my golden years, my visits here are filled with adventure".

Trina didn't say anything and had a confused look on her face.

Ruth smiled and said, "I know you don't understand, but if you are brave enough, you will see." Ruth walked off while Trina stood there for a second, trying to figure out what just happened. Since the sun was down now, Trina made her way back to the house.

When Trina got home, her mind spun with Ruth's words. She couldn't shake it off and decided to take a shower and relax for the night. As she was getting ready for bed, there was a knock on the door. Trina paused and said, "Aw hell naw," under her breath. Thinking there was no way she was answering the door. She waited awhile to make sure she didn't see anyone outside to peek out and make sure her car was cool. When Trina opened the door, there was a package on her doorstep with antique keys and a mysterious note. The note said, "These keys will change your life in unexpected ways."

Trina stood there staring at the box in disbelief. She had no idea what these keys could open or how they could possibly change her life. She slowly reached down to pick up the box and curiously looked inside, only to discover more notes tucked away that revealed these keys were part of something much bigger than just an ordinary set of antique keys.

There were three keys, and each had a note with a location close by and a riddle. Trina felt her heart racing as she walked around the corner. Should she call the police and report what she had seen, or should she give in to her curiosity?

The thought of knowing what was at the first location excited her, but a sense of caution restrained her. With one last deep breath, Trina decided that after breakfast, she would go and see what all the commotion was about. I mean, checking out one of them couldn't hurt, right?

When she woke up, the only thing on her mind was what she was going to find at the first location. Trina went back to the package and picked up the key that had a 1 on it.

She read the clue, and it said "Use the key in the place where nobody has more drip than me." Cheesy, Trina thought as she finished getting ready and left the house for breakfast.

When she got to the spot on the map, she saw a small diner across the street. Trina went in and ordered an omelet and French toast. While she was eating, Trina looked around and said to herself, nobody and nothing around here has any drip! When the waitress came back, Trina asked her if anything near her had any drip? The waitress said, "The only thing that I can think of that drips is the inlet drain across the street by the lake. Trina said, "That must be it"!

Trina rushed over to the inlet drain and saw a gate. She had the key from the package, and she was hoping it was the right one; she inserted it in the lock, and it opened! Trina heard a click and then a loud creak as she stepped inside.

There were crates of what looked like cocaine stacked up on one side and duffle bags of money on the other. Trina's heart raced with excitement; Ruth knew all along that this place was special, but what did she do here? Just then, Trina heard heavy footsteps behind her and quickly turned around to see who it was...

Trina's heart sank as she saw two men in black suits walking towards her. They had stern expressions on their faces and looked intimidating. Trina instinctively took a step back as one of the men spoke. "How did you get in here?" he asked, his voice cold and stern.

Trina tried to compose herself and replied, "I had a key. It was in a package I received."

The man's eyes narrowed, "What package?"

Trina hesitated for a moment, unsure of whether she should reveal the truth. But then she remembered Ruth's words, "You have to be fearless and take risks sometimes." Trina took a deep breath and said, "A package from Ruth."

The two men exchanged a look, and Trina could tell they were deliberating something. Finally, the other man spoke up, "We'll have to take you in for questioning. You understand that, right?"

Trina nodded, feeling a mix of fear and excitement. Trina said to the two, "I need to see a badge first! I think I'm also going live on Insta; ya'll not gon have me on Black Lives Matter"! The man that wasn't talking immediately pulled out a gun.

The quiet man shouted, "This wasn't the deal Ruth."

Trina looked confused as she stood there frozen. "You were supposed to leave it here and never see our face," the man shouted.

Trina shouted, "I ain't Ruth, chill!" as she put her hands up and backed up.

"Who are you then?" the first man shouted! Trina was about to say her name but thought, no way I'm telling them my real name.

Trina shouted, "Kassandra!"

The quiet man said, "You're lying, get your ass on the ground now"! Trina knelt down and faced the wall as she thought to herself this isn't happening.

The first man told the quiet man to watch Trina and go through her purse. As he moved closer, the first man moved towards the money. The quiet man grabbed her purse and was about to snatch it from around her neck, but suddenly let go. Suddenly, the quiet man shouted, "Hey, get away from there!"

Trina turned around to see the two men arguing over the drugs and money. Both men had guns in their hands, pointing at each other, seemingly ready to shoot!

Without thinking, Trina ran out of the drain toward safety. As she ran away, bullets rang out from the drain, but none hit her. She kept running until she was sure that no one was following her. Finally catching her breath, Trina looked up and said a silent thank you, Jesus! Then Trina thought, what the fuck is up with Ruth!

Trina made her way back to the Airbnb, constantly checking to see if anyone was following her like she saw in the movies. When she got inside, she thought she was safe, and it was over. Then her mind got the best of her, and she thought surely they knew where she was staying. They were probably the ones that left the key.

"Shit" Trina shouted as she remembered she had two more keys. She made her way to the package, thinking maybe she should just go home. She picked up the second key and read the clue.

The clue said, "Go to the one that rhymes with and also has the juice." "Ruth" Trina shouted as she darted towards the window.

Trina remembered where she saw her standing and made her way there. She had an uneasy feeling as she walked up to the building, but she kept going. When Trina arrived, she could see that the door was open. She cautiously stepped in and went searching for Ruth.

As Trina made her way through the hallway, it opened up into a large kitchen. Her uneasiness intensified as she saw Ruth standing in the corner of the kitchen with a look of shock on her face. Then, without hesitating, Trina shouted, "Ruth! What is going on here?! What did you do?!"

Ruth was startled to see Trina and said, "Are you here about the deal"? I'm here because of the deal and some people that tried to kill me today! Ruth started questioning Trina about what happened at the drain.

"What were you doing there? Who were those men?" Ruth demanded to know more, but Trina knew that if she told Ruth who those men were, then it would put her in danger, too. So, instead of giving up information, Trina decided to deflect and asked, "What do you mean what was I doing there? Bitch, what are you doing here?" Ruth quipped, "That's classified. All I can say is I am trying to stop Santiago."

Before Trina could ask another question, Ruth said, "If you're here, the plan has changed. Give me the keys and get as far away from here as you can". Ruth moved forward toward Trina, stretching out her hand. Trina thought that Ruth could be lying and ran out of the house towards the garage.

In the garage, she found a tennis racquet. Trina grabbed it and swung into the area behind her, where she heard Ruth running behind her. Ruth hit the wall and fell to the ground. Ruth's eyes widened as she realized what happened. "This bitch really hit me!" Ruth shouted, her voice raising an octave higher than usual.

Trina dropped the tennis racquet and ran out of the garage. She sprinted back to the Airbnb, feeling like she was being chased by a ghost. Trina made it safely inside and locked all the doors and windows. Her heart was racing, her breathing heavy, and she felt like she had just run a marathon. All Trina could think was, what have I gotten myself into?

Trina was in shock and didn't know what to do. She knew if she stayed, she would be in even more danger. Without thinking, Trina ran to start gathering her things. All she knew was that she had to get out of there.

A few moments later, she heard the front door open. A skinny guy walked in; he was of average height and build. Trina turned the bedroom lights out and hid in the closet. The man started to get closer, shouting, "Hello, is anyone here?".

When Trina could hear him outside the closet, she pushed it open as hard as she could. The man fell to the floor, shouting "Hey, what are you doing." Trina ran to the kitchen and grabbed a knife. She quickly turned around and waited for the man to appear. Moments later, the man appeared in the kitchen doorway. He saw the knife and said, "Chill lady, this is all fake"!

It took a second for Trina to process this. Then she noticed the cop car out front with the light flashing. The man said, "My name is Lee; this is all a staged experience." Trina said, "If this is all fake, why are you doing this to me? I didn't ask for this"! Lee said, "We know! My guys got mixed up yesterday when they spotted you and the first actor at the lake. Her name is Ruth; both of those guys are new and thought you were the client. Ruth also thought you were the client and set the experience in motion. Trina had a confused look on her face and said, "The client for what?" Lee said, "The client for the secret agent experience."

Lee went on to explain that he ran a tourist company that used actors to let people feel like they were something they weren't. The guys thought she was the new client Kierra that day at the lake and left her the package on accident. They got suspicious when she didn't finish the scene down at the drain, and Kierra called wanting her money back.

Trina was supposed to take one of the guns and shoot her way out. The bullets in the guns were blanks. The police were there now because she started her Insta live, and it had been running since she left the drain. Some of her followers called the police. Apparently, her phone was sticking out of her back pocket enough for them to see where she was. This also means that they saw a lot and heard everything.

Trina left Stone Mountain that day, thankful that she was safe and in no trouble. All she could think to herself was adventure hits different when you didn't ask for it. Also, people were talking about her now based on her live broadcast. It didn't help that she broke Ruth's collarbone in their little altercation.

In the coming weeks, Trina would get something else she didn't ask for. Trina was getting canceled on social media for hitting that old lady and breaking into that house. Trina reached out to Ruth to apologize again and see if there was anything she could do. This fifth time, Ruth felt like Trina was going through something and told her to call Pastor Morrison. That is how Trina ended up at church today! Thinking to herself, was this all worth it? Trina said to herself, "Next time, imma stay home and binge-watch The Office."

CHAPTER TWO
Fast Money Hit Different

The late August sun bore down relentlessly on the large campus of Northwood University, where Chyla Jackson stepped into her bedroom. Her full chest undulating nervously in her pink t-shirt that was two sizes too small.

Chyla had barely settled into her new college life when she found herself caught in the whirlwind of chaos and temptation. It was only her second week on campus, but she was already feeling the financial strain. Her scholarship covered tuition, but the cost of living, textbooks, and everything else was piling up faster than she could manage.

She wanted to have nail tech appointments and wear the prettiest wigs to class, like her roommate, Tamika. But the money was just as fine as the strands of her Peruvian hair.

Chyla's side of the room was adorned with bright pink walls and framed posters of influential black women, from Maya Angelou to Michelle Obama.

She had claimed the corner closest to the window, allowing sunlight to bathe her space in a warm, inviting glow.

On the opposite side of the room, separated by a whimsical beaded curtain, was her roommate Tamika's territory. Tamika was the very picture of affluence, with her sleek designer outfits and an air of sophistication that seemed out of place in their modest dorm room.

Chyla couldn't help but be intrigued by the contrast between their two worlds.

Tamika was always impeccably dressed in designer clothes, with jewelry that gleamed as if it had been plucked from a high-end boutique. She had a penchant for expensive makeup and the latest gadgets. Chyla couldn't help but wonder how Tamika managed to maintain such a lavish lifestyle.

Just as Chyla stepped out of her tight blue jeans, she overheard a heated phone conversation between Tamika and her father. The earlier silence had led her to presume that she was all alone.

"No, Dad, you don't understand," Tamika's voice was strained as she ripped her earbuds out her ear. Chyla knew Tamika was probably jamming away to loud music again. "I told you I need that money. It's important!"

Chyla couldn't make out her father's words, but it was clear he was trying to explain something.

"I don't care about your business deals, Dad! You promised me. You said I would finally be getting my allowance this week!"

As the conversation grew more heated, Chyla began to piece together the situation. Tamika's father was apologizing for not being able to send her allowance this week, and it sounded like this wasn't the first time it had happened.

Chyla's mind raced as she processed the implications. Tamika wasn't the wealthy heiress she appeared to be. Instead, she seemed to be struggling with financial issues of her own. It was a revelation that made Chyla reevaluate her initial assumptions about everything.

The next day, Chyla decided to confront Tamika about what she had overheard. They were sitting in their room, the afternoon sun casting long shadows through the pink curtains as they shared a cheap bottle of whiskey.

"Tamika," Chyla began cautiously, "I couldn't help but hear your conversation with your dad last night."

Tamika's expression shifted from surprise to guarded. "What did you hear?"

Chyla chose her words carefully. "It sounded like you were having money troubles."

"Yeah, you heard right. My dad's going through some tough times with his business, and he hasn't been able to send my allowance for quite a while," Tamika sighed, her shoulders slumping.

Chyla nodded, and the question bothering her mind finally spilled out. "I thought you said Daddy paid for these and those too." An accusing finger was pointed at a blue shopping bags in the corner.

"Yeah, daddy did. Not my dad, my daddy." Tamika raised an eyebrow, doubling over in laughter as understanding dawned on Chyla.

Tamika had a sugar daddy!
Chyla hesitated for a moment before asking, "Is it that lucrative?"

"More than you can imagine, these rich men honestly don't care about card limits."

Chyla leaned in, her voice lowered as if her words would bite. "Could you put me on?"

"Sure, gurl. They'll love you at Dionysus." Tamika nodded fast, long black curls bouncing around her ebony skin.

Tamika wasted no time in dolling Chyla up in the skimpiest black dress she owned. Her curvy body jiggled in the thin fabric as she wobbled into the club. Tamika had called her a moneymaker as she laid the edges of one of her expensive wigs on her. She knew why now as eyes gravitated to her from all corners of the loud club.

"Hey, shortcake," The bouncer at the VIP gate held the velvet ropes open with a familiar smile to Tamika.

"Hey, hot stuff," She blew him a kiss, walking up the stairs in her sparkly silver dress. Her heart-shaped face shimmered underneath strobe lights, and her red lips pulled into an automatic smile. "Look who missed me!"

A group of older men with obvious wedding bands on their ring fingers offered instant smiles to Chyla. Their crisp suits, gelled salt and pepper hair with the orange glow of cigars overwhelmed her as her bubbly roommate sat right between them on a leather couch.

"You brought a friend." A deep voice replied from the side, sending shivers up Chyla's spine. His face blurred behind a curtain of smoke, leaving only his piercing blue eyes to her gaze.

"Come here, Chy. They don't bite."

Chyla nervously moved over to the table, settling at the edge of the couch. The bottles of alcohol in ice buckets and full ashtrays on the glass table between them overwhelmed her. She had been to her fair share of clubs with her boyfriend back in Denver, but never like this one.

"What's your name?" The deep voice jolted Chyla again, sending a mix of attraction and fear through her.

The luxurious shopping bags flashed in her mind, and she realized this wasn't the place for blushing or getting shy. "Chyla. You can call me yours. I don't really mind."

"Oh really?" The man with blue eyes chuckled, beckoning her over with a smile. "I'm Zion. I like you."

The straightforward confession made Chyla wobble in her heels. But this was Dionysus, a hub of hedonistic behavior and debauchery. She had just found herself a sugar daddy.

~~~~~~~~~

"Damn, Girl. Zion is a spender spender. That bag costs almost sixteen grand." Tamika exclaimed as Chyla unpacked yet another box.

It had been a week since Chyla's first day at Dionysus, and Zion had been nothing but generous. He spent lavishly on Chyla, who now wore the best wigs and the best clothes.

"He tried. I told him I wanted it in blue or black, and he got both." Chyla walked up to the mirror, checking the bag out from all angles. She put her cell phone into it, trying to gauge how much stuff would fit in there.

Her movements paused as her finger hit a hard object in the bag. "What's this?"

"What you mean?" Tamika asked, getting off Chyla's wrapper-covered bed.

"I don't know... it's an invitation?" The astonishment in Chyla's voice was loud and clear as she carefully scrutinized the large white card in her hands.

"Come to my house. 23.03.23."

Chyla let out a heavy sigh, flinging the bag and its contents onto the bed. She had known Zion would do this again. He had spent a lot of their time together trying to convince her to come to his home in Beverly Hills.

Tamika picked up the invitation and hissed, tossing it onto the bed again. "I thought I told you to tell him no."

"I did." Chyla groaned, rubbing the spot between her perfectly tamed brows. "He just won't take a hint. Should I just go?"

"No!" Tamika glanced at Chyla like she had lost her mind and everything in between. "We laugh and drink with them, nothing more. No going to their homes and stuff. He's married!"

Chyla nodded in agreement, but her eyes lingered a little longer on the invite card. Zion took care of her but held her at arm's length. She wanted more, not just cash to be comfortable; she wanted to be rich.

~~~~~~~~~~

Ding dong.

Five days later and against better advice, Chyla stood in front of large Oakwood doors after spending the entire day at the waxers, giving Tamika the excuse of preparing for her upcoming English exams.

"Look who we have here. Come on in." Zion greeted as he swung the door open. Loud music blared from inbuilt speakers in the luxurious interior.

Chyla awkwardly adjusted her short blue dress. She knew it was going to be a grand home, but this level of luxury blew her mind. Chandeliers hung from high ceilings, casting a warm glow on paintings that definitely cost an arm and a leg.

As her eyes scanned the room, they landed on a series of framed photographs adorning the walls. Her heart skipped a beat when she saw them – pictures of Zion, smiling brightly, with a stunning woman by his side.

Chyla tried to ignore the images, reminding herself that her presence here had a specific purpose – to secure her financial future without becoming emotionally entangled. She had to keep her focus on being his sugar baby, nothing more.

Zion led her upstairs, and her heart raced with every step. She had been clear about her boundaries, and she hoped he understood that she wasn't here for a romantic relationship. She was determined to maintain that boundary, no matter how tempting the luxurious lifestyle might be.

As they reached the top of the staircase, Zion opened a door, revealing a beautiful office. Chyla stepped inside, her eyes widening at the sight of it. The room was filled with expensive furniture, a massive mahogany desk, and a floor-to-ceiling bookshelf lined with leather-bound volumes.

But her awe was short-lived, heart plummeting as she laid eyes on the last thing she expected to find in that room – Zion's wife. She was sitting behind the desk, elegant and poised, her gaze fixed on Chyla.

The older woman was breathtakingly beautiful, with silver-streaked ebony hair cascading down her shoulders and a presence that filled the room. Her green eyes, however, held a steely resolve that sent a shiver down Chyla's spine.

"Zion, dear, you're back early," his wife said with a cool smile, her voice dripping with honeyed charm.

Zion cleared his throat, shifting uncomfortably. "Yes, I am, Emily. I... I have someone I'd like you to meet."

Chyla's mind spun as she tried to process the situation. She had assumed she would be discreetly meeting with Zion, away from prying eyes. Now, standing in the presence of his wife, she felt exposed and vulnerable.

Zion's wife, Emily, extended a manicured hand toward Chyla. "I'm Emily, and you must be..."

Chyla swallowed hard, her voice trembling slightly as she replied, "I'm Chyla."

Emily's smile remained fixed, but her eyes seemed to bore into Chyla's soul. "Chyla, it's lovely to meet you. Zion has mentioned you before. He's told me all about your...arrangement."

Chyla's cheeks burned with embarrassment. She hadn't anticipated this level of transparency. She shifted her weight from one foot to the other, desperately wishing she could disappear.

"I hope you understand, Chyla," Emily continued, "that in this house, we value honesty and trust above all else. You're not the first, nor will you be the last."

Chyla nodded, unable to find her voice. Her heart was pounding in her chest, and her mind was racing. Meeting the wife wasn't exactly on her to-do list for the day.

Zion placed his hands heavily on her shoulders, whispering into her ears. "Don't be so tense sweetheart. Let's have dinner."

His strong hand guided Chyla and Emily down the grand staircase with polished oak banisters. As they entered the dining room, Chyla's eyes widened in awe. The long mahogany table was adorned with fine china, crystal glasses, and gleaming silverware. A bouquet of fresh flowers sat in the center, brightening up the room.

Emily gracefully took her seat at the head of the table while Zion gestured for Chyla to sit next to him. Chyla hesitated, gauging Emily's reaction from the corner of her eye.

The dinner Emily had prepared was a gourmet feast. The aroma of roasted meats, exotic spices, and rich sauces filled the room. Chyla's suspicions grew as she realized that a meal of this magnitude should have required an entire kitchen staff, yet no other servants were in sight.

With trepidation, Chyla picked up her fork and began to eat. The meat was exquisite, melting in her mouth with every bite, but she couldn't shake the feeling that something was off. Her eyes darted between Emily and Zion, who watched her intently as they sipped red wine.

Finally, Emily broke the silence. "You know, Zion, she really is perfect."

Chyla swallowed her bite of food and raised an eyebrow, her unease growing. "Perfect for what?"

Emily exchanged a knowing glance with Zion before she leaned in closer to Chyla. "Chyla, we have a proposition for you. It's unconventional, but we believe it could be mutually beneficial."

Chyla's heart raced as she set her fork against the plate with a clank. She had never imagined that her meeting with Zion would lead to such a bizarre and unsettling situation with his wife.

Zion cleared his throat and spoke with a serious tone. "Emily and I, we want to have a child, but not just any child. We've always dreamt of having a black baby. A baby that is both of ours."

Chyla's eyes widened, and she almost choked on her food. She couldn't believe what she was hearing. It sounded like a twisted joke, but the earnest expressions on their faces told her otherwise.

"You want me to…" Chyla stammered, unable to finish her sentence.

Emily nodded, her voice unwavering. "Yes, Chyla. We want you to carry our child. I did my research immediately. Zion told me about you, and we believe you would be the perfect surrogate."

Chyla had entered this mansion expecting Zion to get all touchy and weird, not to become entangled in a bizarre plan to bear a child for this wealthy couple. Her heart pounded in her chest as she realized that Tamika was right. She should have never agreed to come here.

"I can't do this. Also, surrogacy with a black mother doesn't automatically guarantee a black child," Chyla finally managed to say, her voice trembling. "This is... it's too much and impossible."

Zion reached out and placed a reassuring hand on her shoulder. His voice sounded like a hammer pounding into her skull. "Chyla, think about it. We'll give you money beyond your wildest dreams. We'll take care of everything – medical expenses, a comfortable living arrangement, and generous compensation. You'll be well taken care of, and our child will have the best life imaginable."

Chyla's head was spinning. She knew they weren't dumb. The baby would be as white as snow with no influence from her own genes. "Zion, Emily, with all due respect, it's impossible. It's only if it's my baby through and through that it'll have a…..darker skin tone."

A part of her felt offended at the proposition. This was probably why Zion was so generous and lavish with his spending. Her hands sneakily tapped at her phone underneath the table, sending out an urgent text to Tamika.

I'm really sorry I lied to you. I'll send you my location, these white people done lost their goddamn minds!

"We'll keep trying until a miracle happens. I believe it's possible." Emily gave a rigid smile, downing the rest of her red wine.

Chyla was close to blowing a fuse; Zion and Emily sounded like broken record players that grated on her nerves. "Listen, lady, it's medically impossible for a surrogate mother to pass her genes to the baby. So, if you want to use your egg and his sperm. It's gonna be a white ass baby."

Zion slammed his fist on the table, giving me a harsh glare. "That's enough, Chyla." His blue eyes held nothing but anger now as he rose to his feet.

"So you want to sleep with my husband?"

"What? No!" Chyla exclaimed, flabbergasted by the sudden turn of events. "I'm just pointing out the facts. Dinner was lovely, but I'll take my leave now."

Chyla felt her knees wobble as she stood up from the dining table. She was in way over her head now, and it was time to leave crazy-ville.

Zion's anger was evident in his clenched fists and the stern look in his eyes. Emily's demeanor had shifted as well, her elegant poise replaced by a more assertive stance. Chyla knew she had touched a nerve with her comments about the impossibility of her passing her genes to their child.

"I think it's best if I leave now," Chyla stated, trying to maintain her composure.

Zion stepped closer, his voice low and menacing. "You can't just walk out of here, Chyla. You're in too deep now."

Chyla's heart raced as she realized she might be in a dangerous situation. She had no idea how far Zion and Emily were willing to go to achieve their impossible goal.

Suddenly, the room seemed to close in on her. Chyla glanced at the door, considering making a run for it, but Zion was blocking her path. Panic welled up inside her, and she desperately needed help.

That's when her phone buzzed discreetly in her palm. It was Tamika's response to her urgent text.

Tamika: "Girl, you gotta get outta there! I'm on my way."

Chyla's eyes flicked back to Zion, who was now just inches away, his anger simmering. She knew she had to make a move before things got worse.

In one swift motion, Chyla lunged towards the door, attempting to squeeze past Zion. He grabbed her arm, and for a moment, they struggled in a tense standoff.

"Let me go!" Chyla pleaded, fear coursing through her veins.

Just then, loud knocks echoed through the living room. Someone was at the door. Emily rose to her feet and opened the door. The front door was barely open halfway before it burst open, and Tamika stormed into the room. Her eyes were wide with concern as she looked for her roommate. "What's going on here?"

Zion released his grip on Chyla and turned to face Tamika. "What the hell are you doing here Tamika?"

"I'm her very worried roommate and friend," Tamika replied firmly. "And I'm here to make sure she's safe."

Chyla quickly moved towards Tamika, putting some distance between herself and Zion. The tension in the room was thick, but with Tamika by her side, Chyla felt a glimmer of hope.

Zion, realizing the wide open door and the feisty woman, took a step back, his craze still evident in his eyes. "Fine, leave. But remember, Chyla, you've heard our proposition. We're willing to make it worth your while."

Chyla nodded, her heart pounding. She knew she had narrowly escaped a potentially dangerous situation. "I'll consider it," she replied, not wanting to provoke them further. She knew she wasn't going to consider shit.

As they stepped out into the night, Chyla couldn't help but feel relieved to be away from that place. She had entered this house for some quick money, but this was beyond her depths. They were crazy and needed psychiatric help.

Tamika, her savior, put a reassuring hand on Chyla's shoulder. "Girl, we need to have a serious talk about you not listening to my warnings!"

Chyla nodded, her mind still reeling from the events of the evening. It sure hits different when you're way in over your head.

CHAPTER THREE

Choosing Yourself Hits Different!

Maura Williams had anxiously been waiting for her roommate, Suzanne, to come home for the past two hours. She actually feared that she would have to sleep on the street tonight if Suzanne failed to come home.
Suzanne had borrowed her key two days ago when she had lost hers on a date with her married boyfriend. Karma works in mysterious ways. Since then, Maura had to wake up an hour earlier to go to work so she could leave Suzanne to lock up and keep the key.
Maura had been waiting outside the entrance of her shared home with Suzanne for the past two hours. She had texted Suzanne on the phone an hour ago, and she had replied that she would be late, as she was still busy with Michael - the married boyfriend.
The night was chilly, and the weather was tethering on the brink of winter. Maura wrapped her fur cardigan around her body to block out the cold as she sat on the balcony steps.
Occasionally, she would look up when she heard the sounds of incoming footsteps, hoping it was her roommate. But the street was almost empty, with only a few passerbys on the road.
Maura's stomach growled loudly, which reminded her that she had yet to grab lunch in the office. One of her colleagues, Nora, had begged her again to help her

work on a document that needed to be faxed to the head of the sales department immediately after lunchtime, so she had had to work on that while Nora rushed off to grab lunch.

She had thought Nora would grab lunch for her, too, but the latter had come back empty-handed. Maura had asked her for her lunch, but she had shrugged like Maura had asked her for something out of the ordinary and then proceeded to demand if the document was ready.

Maura thought Nora might be a little self-absorbed, or maybe she was imagining it because she was never that way with other people in the office. She hissed, shaking her legs to regain feeling while texting Suzanne again.

"I'm still waiting outside, Su, and I'm starving."

The message showed two blue ticks, notifying her that it had been delivered and read. She waited for a reply, anxiously staring at her phone, but a reply never came. She looked up from the phone and noticed a woman across the street staring intently at her.

Maura became afraid and wondered if she was in danger.

The woman started walking towards her, and Maura contemplated running into the house, but when she remembered that it was locked, she stayed put.

"Hello miss," the woman said. She was African American with the most glorious black hair Maura had ever seen. She was a bit on the light side, with at least three tattoos on her bare arms and one on the back of her palm. She was a beautiful woman.

"Hello," Maura replied, enchanted by the woman, albeit a little wary.

"I'm Jessie; I live in the next building," The woman said, offering her hand to Maura.

Maura took it. "I'm Maura; nice to meet you."

"I noticed you have been sitting outside in the cold for the past two days, and I do not feel right seeing you sit all by yourself alone at night. The neighborhood may not be known for its high crime rate, but that doesn't mean it doesn't happen once in a while, you know," Jessie said, her brown eyes full of worry.

Maura felt her heart warm all over at the woman's concern for her and almost burst into tears.

"Thanks, Jessie, I'm waiting for my roommate."

Jessie's eyes clouded over with confusion. "Your roommate? Don't you have a key to the apartment?"

"Oh, I do. But my roommate, Suzanne, that's her name, lost hers, and she has to use mine, you see." Maura explained that the situation was the most obvious thing in the world.

Jessie was silent for a long while, staring at Maura in foolish wonder.

"So, you gave your key to your friend so she could lock you outside and keep you in the cold for hours even though she was the one who was careless with her key?"

Maura avoided her intensive stare and shrugged, embarrassed.

She guessed that she would, of course, look like a fool to a complete stranger who did not know her roommate and didn't know how cranky she could get when she didn't have her way.

Maura would rather look like a fool than say no to people. People always said she was very nice. She always wondered if it was praise or an insult.

"Will she be back anytime soon then?" Jessie asked

"Oh, she should be back soon. She just texted me that she is on her way," Maura lied.

Jessie nodded, though it was evident that she didn't believe her.

They were both silent for a while.

"Let me wait with you till she comes." Jessie bent down, sitting on the stairs with her.
"Oh no, there is no need to go to all that trouble for me; she will soon be here, I'm sure!" Maura was now a little bit alarmed, afraid that Suzanne would not come soon and her lie would be uncovered.
Jessie stood up reluctantly. "Okay, if you say so." There was an indecisive note in her tone.
Maura smiled and thanked her again profusely.
Jessie nodded and started to walk away, then she turned back abruptly after taking a few steps. "You know, you should choose yourself once in a while," and then walked away into the darkness.
Maura continued peering at the retreating figure of the woman in confusion until she disappeared from sight.
"Choose yourself once in a while. What does she mean by that?" Maura wondered.
Thirty minutes later, she heard the click-clack of heels on the asphalt of the street. She looked up and saw Suzanne coming, no, swaying towards the building. Maura quickly ran to catch her before she fell.
"Suzanne, what is the matter…" She paused, catching a strong whiff of alcohol from her curvy roommate. "Oh, you are drunk; come, let's go in." She guided her roommate to the door while rummaging through her bag.
Suzanne held onto her loosely while she searched for the keys. She found it and opened the door to let them into the apartment.
The warmth of the sitting room was heaven compared to the cold outside. Maura switched on the lights and arranged Suzanne on their pastel-colored couch. The room was in disarray; pillows were scattered around, and the TV remote was lying on the floor.
When she had left for work, the room had been in pristine condition since she had taken pains to clean

everywhere after the party Suzanne had thrown the night before, which had left everywhere grossly untidy with cigarette butts, beer cups, and someone's vomit on the rug.

Now, Suzanne must have made it untidy again after she had left.

Maura sighed, tired and hungry. She intended to wait to start tackling the mess. All she wanted to do was eat and go to sleep.

She went to the fridge and opened it to see what she could eat, and to her surprise, there was nothing but a half-eaten box of cereal.

She had stocked the fridge just two days ago, and now everything was gone. She closed the fridge angrily and went to sit.

Suzanne and her party friends must have finished everything yesterday. She longed to shake Suzanne until she rattled, but she was too docile and too hungry to do so.

Instead, she sobbed softly, frustrated with the situation and angry with Suzanne. It didn't help that she had used her last paycheck to buy the groceries. Now, she wouldn't have a choice but to dip her hands in her savings tomorrow.

She stood up wearily, got the cereal out of the fridge, and ate it unhappily. As she descended into sleep that night, the last thing she could think about was Jessie's words, "Choose yourself once in a while."

Maura woke up late the next morning and prepared for work hurriedly. On her way out, Maura met Suzanne seated on the couch watching TV in a sheer nightgown that accentuated her curves, and her heavy mass of red hair flowed around her.

"Good morning, Su," Maura grunted.

"Could you lend me a hundred?" Su asked, not even bothering to reply to the greeting.

Maura's heart sank. *'not even an apology about yesterday or thank you.'*
Nonetheless, She dipped her hands in her purse and gave Su the money, regret tying her stomach in knots.

~~~~~~~~~

Two hours later, she got to her office. Maura worked as a copy editor at Bernhardt Publishing, one of the most prestigious publishing companies in New York.
The smell of newly printed books wafted up her nose as she entered the office. She greeted her colleagues and settled down to work.
"Good morning, Maura" Nora called, smiling at her as she walked towards Maura's desk, her feet delicately fitting into white stilettos.
Everyone agreed that Nora was the most beautiful woman in the company. She was tall and curvy and had the wildest mane of dark hair that she loved putting in a ponytail. Her looks were more fitting on a runway than a publishing house, yet she never looked out of place. Maura always felt dowdy next to her.
Max, the handsome office rake and Maura's longtime crush, also seemed to harbor some kind of affection for Nora, and she, in turn, was completely besotted with him.
Maura wondered what Nora wanted since she was being so nice. Nora was only friendly to her when she needed something from her.
"Morning Nora," She replied warily.
Nora leaned on her desk and tapped it with a manicured fingernail.
"Um, Maura darling," Nora whined, grating on Maura's nerves.
"Could you do me a favor?" Maura's heart sank at Nora's question.

What a way to begin a day,
"What do you want, Nora?" Maura asked wearily
"There is this manuscript giving me a serious headache; I was hoping you could help me with it," she complained, touching her palm to her forehead in feigned distress.

Maura wanted to tell her that she couldn't, but the words lodged in her mouth and would not come out. Finally, she swallowed her refusal and nodded. Nora clapped her hands excitedly like a child that had just been given candy and sashayed back to her desk to grab the manuscript. Her manicured hands dumped the manuscript on Maura's desk and disappeared.

Maura gazed at nothing in particular at first, embarrassed at her inability to say no to someone who was obviously using her.

"Hey, Maura." A deep masculine voice called her out of her musings. It was Max, looking even more handsome than he looked yesterday in a dapper grey suit and shiny black Italian shoes.

Maura blushed very hard and smiled. "Good morning Max."

Max went into his office and closed it behind him. He was the editor-in-chief, so he got to have an office to himself. A rumor went that he came from a wealthy family with ancestral ties to the Windsors.

That was probably the main reason why Nora was determined to have him for herself. Maura quickly discarded all thoughts of Max from her mind. After all, there was no use for it since they were both worlds apart in looks and status.

A few hours later, she got up from her desk to get some food. She took the elevator and walked out of the building to a nearby diner. The manager, Lucas, knew her and made a gesture to her to sit and wait for him.

She sat down in a corner booth and brought out her phone to check her messages. She saw that her nineteen-year-old younger brother, Tio, had already texted her several times to call him. She hoped he wasn't calling to complain about their mother or to ask for money again.

Maura's mother was a recovering addict, and Maura had grown up cleaning her mother's mess and had single-handedly brought up her younger brother, who was five years her junior. She dialed his number, and he picked up on the first ring.

"Hey, saw your texts, what's up?" she asked, mouthing her thanks to Lucas, who had brought her usual order of bacon, eggs, and latte.

"Hey, I wanted to remind you about the money you promised me last week; you know Mama collected the last one from me," Tio grumbled.

Maura rubbed her forehead and bloodshot eyes as a headache began to set in. "Well, you didn't tell me that she did," she scolded lightly, betraying the anger she felt at her mom. At the whole fucking world at large.

"um.... well she did." Tio sounded a little concerned, worried that his sister wouldn't respond like he expected.

"Fine, I'll call her," Maura promised.

"Okay, but what about the money, then?" he asked again.

"I will send it to you very soon." But Maura was wondering how she would survive after she wiped out her savings.

'How soon?" Tio demanded rudely.

"Today," Maura said, and her brother ended the call without as much as a goodbye.

Maura sighed, hating herself for giving in yet again to pressure. Her brother was a darling to her, but she did not fail to notice that he had inherited their mother's selfishness. Tio never called her except to ask for money. Her mother called her frequently to ask for favors, berate her, and guilt trip her for leaving home to go to college.

She didn't spare a thought that she might not have any money to give if she hadn't gone to college and gotten a suitable job. Maura hurriedly finished her food and paid.

On getting to the office, she decided to go to the restroom to fix her appearance. As she got to the entrance, she heard her name being mentioned in a conversation coming from the toilet. Curious, she hid herself so she could listen in on the conversation.

"She sure is a dense one, isn't she?" a voice Maura recognized as one of the illustrators said.

"Yeah, she is. But her dumbness works fine with me. All I need to do is flick my fingers, call Maura, and she does what I ask of her." Nora giggled, and the other girl followed suit.

"She is too nice, what a loser!" the illustrator said, disdain dripping from her voice as Nora laughed again.

Maura felt blood drain from her face as she listened. Is that what everyone thought of her? That she was some dumb and extra nice loser? She felt her headache grow, and she fought the tears gathering in her eyes. As she turned around to take to her heels, her eyes met Max's, who was standing outside the gents and was staring intently at her with something that looked like a mixture of compassion and anger.

She felt doubly embarrassed with herself, for she was sure that he heard every disgusting thing those girls said about her. A surge of anger rose in her, and she fought to control it.

She fled downstairs and ran out of the building, finally letting her tears flow fast and free. Maura walked a while and finally sat in a nearby park and watched absentmindedly as children ran around with dogs and lovers and cuddled together on the grass. She watched the happiness of other people with a pang of envy. What she would give to have happiness like theirs, she thought.

She felt someone watching her, looked in the direction of the stare, and saw Jessie, the woman she met yesterday night, sitting just a few steps from her. Maura waved, and she waved back, walking up to her.

"Hey, fancy meeting you here," Maura said.

Jessie smiled and shrugged. Then she gave Maura a once over and said, "You look so sad."

Maura laughed dryly. "I guess I am....that thing you said yesterday about me choosing myself," she said, gazing intently at Jessie.

"What about it?" Jessie asked, lacing her fingers together and crossing her legs.

"I think I finally understand it," Maura said softly, looking away at a faraway distance.

"Jessie, all my life, I've let people walk all over me and take from me without ever giving back. My mum, my brother, my roommate, my colleagues at work, even my exes...I have always wondered why I let them do it, but now I know," Maura bitterly smiled.

"Why do you let them do it?" Jessie asked, taking Maura's palms and enclosing them in hers in a bid to give her comfort.

"I think part of the reason is that I have had to be responsible for myself and others from a young age, responsible for my drug addict mother and my younger brother, and I have grown used to it to the extent that I have made other people's needs come first."

Jessie nodded. "You need to love yourself, Maura, and refuse to be used; until you do that, you will continue to be sad."

Maura's eyes shone with anger and determination. "It will change from now on. I will never let anyone use me again."

~~~~~~~~~

An hour later, she was back at the office. She put aside Nora's manuscript and faced her own work squarely while eagerly anticipating Nora's confrontation.

"Maura dear, are you done with my manuscript?" Nora asked an hour later, in a patronizing tone, strutting towards Maura's desk.

Maura itched to slap her face but controlled her temper and looked up at Nora calmly. "No, Nora, I haven't, and I don't intend to."

"What do you mean you haven't, Maura?" Nora faltered, unsure about what to do with this unusual Maura

Maura stood up and hit the table furiously. "I said you can go fuck yourself, Nora." She challenged, tone as cold as the Arctic.

Nora's eyes widened with shock, and then she looked around and saw that everyone's eyes were fixed on the commotion, and she reddened with embarrassment. Maura did not care. She took her seat and pointed to the manuscript. "Take that and go," she commanded Nora. Nora took it and walked away hurriedly, and Maura sighed with relief. She looked up and noticed Max watching her from the door of his office with a pleased smile and a thumbs up sign; she glowed with joy.

Maura walked home with a bounce in her steps and texted Suzanne, "I am home. Bring my key NOW." She hoped the tone of the text would make Suzanne arrive fast. Five minutes later, Su approached the apartment angrily.

"What the fuck was that text Maura?"

Maura was not fazed by her reaction. In fact, she expected it.

"I meant exactly what I said, Su; I want my key," She sniped, grinning inwardly at Suzanne's incredulous stare.

"What has come over you?" Suzanne asked weakly.

"Nothing but the realization that you are a very selfish person, and I am not interested in letting you use me anymore. Now let me have your two months' rent and my key..." she demanded and stretched forth her hand.

Suzanne paused, contemplating whether to call Maura's bluff; she decided against it as she saw that Maura wasn't backing out.

"Fine!" she growled and handed the keys to Maura. "I will give you the money tomorrow morning" she promised heatedly and then added as an afterthought, disappointment dripping from her tone, "You are not a nice person, Maura."

"Yes! I would take that over being too nice" Maura shit back, opened the door, and started to go to her room, then turned around dramatically. "Oh, lest I forget, I would appreciate it if you returned the groceries I bought with my money. You can keep the hundred dollars; consider it the last of my charity." She finished triumphantly and went into her room, leaving Suzanne gasping in shock.

~~~~~~~~~~~

Weeks later, everyone knew that Maura was a new person. She had dinner once a week with Jessie, who had become a close friend and confidant. To top it all, Max had given Nora the cold shoulder publicly and asked Maura out.

She had told her brother to get a job and warned her mother to never call her to berate her ever again, or she would cut her off completely. The both of them were left speechless at her firmness, which had given Maura a stab of warm satisfaction.

Saying no sure hits different when all you have been doing is saying yes.

CHAPTER FOUR

Betrayal Hits Different!

Imani had always thought her husband of ten years was the best thing since sliced bread. Even when most of their peers had fallen out of love with each other after the children came, Imani thought she and Kyle were still very much in love after three beautiful kids. Imani and Kyle had met in college. She was the shy geek, while Kyle was the handsome jock that most of the girls crushed on. Imani had also nursed her crush for him, but she hadn't deluded herself that Kyle would like her when she knew he had a plethora of beautiful girls dying for him.

So when Kyle had chosen her in a frat party game, no one was more surprised than her. She had walked on clouds since then, ignoring the envious stares of the other girls and reveling in Kyle's goodness.

Imani and Kyle began dating soon after and became the campus's number-one couple. Girls had wondered why Kyle chose quiet and shy Imani when he could have had any beautiful, bold, and confident girl he wanted. Boys thought Kyle was lucky to have such a docile girl who thought the world revolved around him. Imani had studied Banking and finance while Kyle had studied law then they both graduated summa cum laude. Their graduation party had been attended by both their families, who already took it for granted that their children would definitely end up married to each other. Kyle and Imani had decided that there would be no need for Imani to use her degree since Kyle would be earning enough as a lawyer to take care of their family financially.

They had gotten married a year after they graduated, and not long after, Kyle was a partner in his firm despite his young age. He was considered the best criminal lawyer in Manhattan. They had everything they had dreamed of. Money, status, a nice family, a big house, and close friends of the same status as them. Life was good, Imani thought contentedly.

It was Keisha, their daughter's birthday today, a hot summer day; the sky was glorious. The kind of day that could make families hold barbecue parties in their gardens and children jump around with the joy that only summertime could bring. Imani woke up in her husband's arms, having slept late the night before because of the preparations being made for Keisha's eighth birthday.

The girl had insisted on having a big birthday party and a pony as a birthday gift. Imani and Kyle had promised to throw her a pool party but had refused to get her a pony, which had then brought about a lot of tantrums. However, the tantrums stopped when it was made known to Keisha that she would have to be responsible for the pony, feed it, and generally care for it. Keisha then lost the desire to have a pony, for she did not consider the responsibility fun at all.

She later settled for a visit to Disneyland, which had earned her scoffs from her elder twin brothers, Zayn and Zephyr, who considered Disneyland girly and beneath them.

Imani had invited some of their friends who had young children like theirs. Top on the list were the Delinskys. Robert Delinsky was Kyle's best friend for many years, even before college. They were both top lawyers, with Robert specializing in family law.

Robert and his wife had two adorable twin girls who were Keisha's age mates and besties. Imani's parents were also coming down from Buffalo. Kyle's parents could not come because they were currently on a cruise ship, which had presently docked in Athens, Greece. They had sent Keisha an enormous Barbie house, though.

Imani yawned loudly, thinking about the mountain of tasks she had to handle today. She hoped Martha would come early; she could really use her help. Martha and Imani had grown to become very close friends since they both married best friends. Robert always joked that they didn't have a choice but to be.

"Hey babe," Kyle yawned and cuddled Imani. Imani struggled to release herself from his hold unsuccessfully.

"Babe, let me go; I have things to do," she protested, twisting her body here and there.

Kyle gathered her into his warm embrace and kissed her. Imani felt desire rise in her. Another good thing about their marriage was the fact that they still had the hots for each other. She never refused Kyle sex because he knew all her zones that made her a moaning mess in seconds.

She knew that this wasn't the case with most couples. Martha had once told her that she and Robert hardly had sex anymore. Imani had given a superior smile when Martha told her and offered thanks to God for giving her a perfect husband.

Imani wrapped her arms around her husband's neck and returned his kiss with ardor, and Kyle groaned with pleasure.

"Mommy, Daddy, wake up!" Keisha shouted, bounding into the room excitedly. The lovebirds disengaged faster than lightning. Keisha stopped at the foot of her parents' king sized bed to study them suspiciously, wrinkling her small, cute nose.

"Were you kissing just now?" she asked, displaying wisdom far above her age. Imani and Kyle shook their heads, guilt written all over them.

"I think you have been kissing." Keisha declared and ran out, calling on her brothers to come see what she had discovered.

Imani and Kyle burst into laughter. "Now, that was your fault, babe." Imani accused her husband and stood up to get ready for the day, thanking God she got her braids done last week.

"This is far from over." Kyle wiggled his forefinger at her, and Imani ruffled his thick brown hair affectionately.

An hour later, they were all downstairs; the boys played rough and teased Keisha by pulling her ponytails.

"Stop that Zephyr, stop teasing your sister," Imani warned, overseeing the rest of the preparations with Stella, Kyle's secretary.

"I heard you and Daddy were kissing. Is that right?" Zayn stopped in his tracks, mischief glinting in his eyes.

"None of your business, Zayn," said Kyle, gathering the colored balloons that would be going into the pool in his hands.

Zephyr made kissing sounds, and Zayn joined him. Kyle sputtered with mock anger. "Oh, y'all are gonna get it now, continue." He dropped the balloons and beat his chest like a gorilla, which made the kids giggle, and Imani smiled indulgingly.

The housekeeper and the children's nanny, Mrs. Smith, walked in. "The caterers are here already, Mrs. Miller."

"Okay, please, could you take the kids with you?" Imani pushed the little devils towards her while they protested.

"I don't want you underfoot while I put things in order for the party, kids, so up you go," She ordered.

Mrs Smith marched the reluctant kids upstairs, and Imani heaved a sigh of relief. "When are Robert and Martha coming, darling?" she asked her husband.

"Oh, they should be here anytime from now. Robert just texted me." Kyle gathered the balloons and made for the door.

"Okay, the barbecue, babe, don't forget," Imani called out as he went.

While she was speaking with the caterers, Martha arrived with her husband and the twins, Jade and Jasmine. Martha was a petite woman and was extremely beautiful, intelligent, and funny. She could make a roomful of sour people laugh and unwind, which made her great company at parties. Imani was happy that she came.

"Hey, thanks for coming." She hugged Martha and planted a chaste kiss on Robert's shaved cheek. She sent Robert to her husband and led Martha away while the kids ran upstairs eagerly to see the celebrant.

"Have the DJs arrived yet?" Martha asked, gazing around the garden, which was decorated with balloons and a blowup picture of Keisha at the entrance of the house, which made the atmosphere festive.

"Yes, they are setting up over there." Imani pointed to a part of the garden not very far from the pool.

Martha nodded, swinging her arms." Everything is almost ready; what do you need me to do?"

"Just welcome the guests so I can go get the kids ready," Imani pleaded, and Martha nodded with understanding. Imani went upstairs to see the kids.

The girls were in Keisha's room, sitting on Keisha's pink four-poster bed and giggling as they grossly applied powder to their faces. Everything in Keisha's room was pink; even the walls were painted soft pink. It was a beautiful room for a beautiful girl.

"Hey, girls." Imani walked into the room and ruffled her daughter's chocolate brown locks. "Let's get you ready, birthday girl."

"Mummy, can I wear false eyelashes today?" Keisha pleaded, making Jasmine and Jade giggle.

Imani pretended to be shocked. "Absolutely not!"

Keisha pouted, but her mother ignored her and went to her closet to bring out a beautiful pink gown she just bought for her. Keisha stopped pouting and jumped off the bed excitedly. Imani put the dress on for her and fixed her hair into two pigtails with two pink butterfly clips.

"My beautiful baby girl." Imani kissed Keisha as a tear escaped her eyes, which made the girls giggle.

She rolled her eyes and led them out of the room and into the boys' room. As usual, the room was in disarray, with clothes thrown everywhere and their toys scattered on the floor. The boys were wearing ninja clothes and were busy with plastic sword fights.

"Zephyr, Zayn, I expect you to be dressed and downstairs in five minutes," Imani commanded.

"Ugh, mom! Can't we just stay here? We don't wanna be in a girly party," Zephyr whined, speaking for the two of them.

"No! It's your sister's birthday, and you will get dressed and come downstairs in five minutes, or I seize your Xbox." she threatened.

They both gasped in shock and started peeling off the ninja clothes hurriedly. *Yeah, that's more like it*, Imani thought and marched the girls downstairs.

~~~~~~~~~~~

The party had already started in full swing. The music filled the air. The guests, including Imani's parents, had arrived and were mingling. When the weather warmed up a little bit more, they would all change into their pool clothes and have fun in the pool.

Everyone agreed that Keisha was a perfect birthday girl, and the presents she received were so many that they filled an empty room. All the children were having fun; even Zephyr and Zayn were not left out.

Kyle was surrounded by his friends, who were mostly lawyers, and Imani and Martha entertained their wives while they all kept an eye on the kids who were playing.

"Imani, You have really outdone yourself, well done." Barbara, one of the wives of Kyle's friend, remarked, admiration in her eyes, and all the women nodded in agreement.

"Oh, it wasn't a big deal at all. Martha helped me with most of it." Imani brushed a loose strand behind her ear shyly, trying to be modest but glowing from the praise.

"Now, don't be modest, Imani; I didn't do much; it was mostly you." Martha countered, nursing a glass of wine. She looked slightly peeved. Imani wondered if she was sick.

"Besides, anybody that could make those rambunctious sons of yours dress up for a party is definitely a Wonder Woman." Martha joked, and everyone laughed. "I have to use the ladies' room. Excuse me for a minute."

Imani nodded, grabbing her wine glass helpfully as her friend walked out of the garden.

In a short while, they all settled down to eat and were served crispy chicken wings smothered in a sweet and tangy homemade barbecue sauce by the servers. The cake, which was chocolate with hazelnut frosting and decorated with nine lit birthday candles, was wheeled in, and Keisha stood behind it, holding the knife gingerly, all smiles. She cut the cake after everyone shouted, "Happy birthday Keisha."

They went to change into their pool clothes shortly after, and the kids jumped excitedly into the pool while the adults supervised.

Imani was happy with the success of the party. She looked around with a smile on her lips. The women were in a group, chatting and also keeping an eye on the swimming children, and the men sat together, laughing boisterously. Imani noticed that Kyle was not among the men.

She had to speak with him about paying the caterers. So, she left the others and went into the house to search for him. He wasn't downstairs, so she went upstairs to their room, but he wasn't there either. She looked in every nook and cranny of the big, five bedroom house they lived in, but he was nowhere to be found.

She decided to go to the shed, which was at the back of the house. He usually went there to escape the noise of the children when they played in the small room he used as a home office.

Imani stopped in her tracks as she heard a noise coming from the shed; it sounded like grunts. What was that sound? She hurried towards it and opened the door of the shed slightly. The sight she saw wasn't what she thought she would ever see in her lifetime. Kyle was pants down and humping a woman who was sitting on a makeshift table, legs wide apart, and was moaning softly with passion. The woman was...Martha. Imani stood rooted with shock at the door. She felt the world crashing down on her and held the door for support to keep herself from falling as darkness descended on her. She woke up to find her clothes and her face soaked with water. She was lying on a couch in the sitting room with her head in her mother's lap.

"She's awake." Grandma Rhodes, Imani's mother, exclaimed.

"Babe! Are you alright?" Kyle rushed to her and took her hand in his, acting all worried for her.

Imani itched to snatch her hand away from him and slap him, but she stopped herself. She couldn't discuss such a sensitive issue in front of her guests, so she allowed him to play the caring husband. Her heartbeat erratically as the image of what she had seen in the shed rushed back at her.

She looked around for Martha and saw her standing nervously among the guests. She fought the tears that were building up in her eyes. She couldn't let the world know what she was feeling.

"*Keep it together, Imani*" she chanted to herself.

She allowed her mother to guide her to sit correctly, then she faced her guests and, assured them that she was fine and told them to go home. They bid her farewell and filed out with their kids. Then Kyle and Robert saw them out while Martha remained, though it was obvious to Imani that she was itching to go, but she couldn't because her husband would still stay.

"Mum, where are the children?" she mumbled.

Her mother rubbed her head softly and replied, "They are upstairs with Mrs. Smith and Grandpa Rudolph."

When Kyle and Robert came back from seeing the guests off, Imani then let out a loud heart wrenching sob that spoke volumes of the pain she was feeling. Kyle stayed rooted to the spot he was in, and Martha made a slight, desperate sound. "Ima—"

Robert and Grandma Rudolph wore confusion on their faces. "Imani, what is the matter? Did something bad happen?" Grandma Rudolph inquired, rubbing her daughter's back and searching for understanding in Kyle's face, but what they saw was something akin to fear.

Imani looked up, her face red and eyes haunted; she pointed to Martha, "Ask this bitch how long she has been sleeping with my husband."

"What!!" Robert gasped, looking from Martha to Kyle in confusion. "What are you talking about, Imani?"

"I saw my husband's pants down, fucking your wife in the shed a while ago, Robert." Imani laughed bitterly. The ensuing silence was sickening.

"Fucking hell!! Martha, is this...is this true?" Robert faced Martha, anger pulsing from every pore of his body; his hands were shaking. He tried to place them on a surface to steady them, but he nervously planted them on his face.

"It was a mistake, Robert; I'm sorry" Martha pleaded, tears in her eyes, her mouth shaking pathetically. Imani had the urge to gouge her eyes with her bare fingers to pass on the pain she was feeling.

"You mean you have been sleeping with your friend's wife and your wife's close friend under her own roof? How despicable of you, Kyle." Grandma Rudolph faced Kyle with an incredulous glare.

"It was a mistake, babe... please," Kyle said pathetically, walking up to his wife and attempting to touch her. She shrugged away from his touch as if she had just been touched by a snake.

"Don't touch me!" Imani shouted in agony and burst into tears. "I thought...I thought you loved me. I thought we were a happy golden family that everyone envied. I gave you everything you wanted, Kyle....how could you rip me apart like this?" She covered her red, puffy face with her palms.

"And you..." She pointed to Martha. "I thought we were friends. Do you have any shame at all, do you?"

"We were never friends, Imani...you never considered me as one, all I was to you was someone to brag to about your little perfect life... don't preach to me about friendship!" Martha exploded, pointing aggressively at Imani with poorly concealed envy and hatred.

Martha mimicked cruelly. "Oh, Kyle loves me so much, oh he fucks me so well, my kids are so perfect....yada yada yada."

"That's enough, Martha!" Both Kyle and Robert rebuked at the same time.

Then Robert faced Kyle. "I don't ever want to see you again, you bastard!" He added furiously, flexing his fist as he stormed off.

"Get out of my house, you ragady bitch.....Now!!!" Imani stood up and pointed to the door. Martha glared at Kyle, expecting him to say something in her defense, but he averted his gaze from her. She snorted and stormed off after her husband.

Silence reigned after their exit, and Grandma Rudolph took her cue to leave the couple alone but not failing to hiss disdainfully at Kyle before she left.

"It isn't the first time you are cheating on me, is it?" Imani softly asked, sitting down slowly like an old woman. She felt empty and drained.

"I have never cheated on you, Imani." Kyle lowered himself to a seat very far from Imani and avoided her gaze.

This told Imani that it wasn't his first time, and neither would it be his last. Her heart squeezed inside her, and she feared she would die due to the agony of having lived a lie all through her marriage.

"Did you even love me at least a little, or was everything a lie?" She brushed a tear from her face.

"I did...I mean, I do!" He sneaked a peek at her to see if she believed him, but he saw that she could see right through him.

"How many times and how many people have you cheated on me with?" She knew there was no point torturing herself like this, but she felt she had to know, or she would go crazy.

"Well..." he began and went silent.

"I see..." Imani stood up, oddly feeling energized. She might never recover from the betrayal, but at least she would no longer answer to the status of being a hoodwinked fool.

"I guess I have to thank Martha for finally peeling the rose-tinted glass from my eyes and curing me of delusions...For the sake of the children, I will keep this under wraps unless you prefer otherwise?" He didn't deserve it, but the kids didn't deserve a broken family either. Even though she was hurt, she would be reasonable for their sake.

"No, please...thank you. Are you divorcing me?" He asked sadly, distress written all over him.

Imani felt nothing but disgust for him.

"No, I am not...I won't subject my kids to such a life changing event. But I think you should move out of our bedroom. We will have to find a lie to tell the kids if they ask. After all, we've all been living a lie; one more lie won't hurt." Imani thought she had to do something to make a statement, but what? She had it and moved towards the closet to retrieve one of the boys' baseball bats. She decided to hit him where it hurt; why should she be the only one in pain today? Imani looked at Kyle and said, "Payback is a bitch, and you owe me." Squaring her shoulders as she walked out on him, she turned back and said, "And I'm just getting started." leaving him alone in the room, she headed straight to

Kyle's trophy room with the bat, thinking to herself……..
Betrayal sure hits different, especially from a person you had nothing but love for.

CHAPTER FIVE

Goodbye's Hit Different When You Are With Someone You Love

Seara longed for the school bell to ring as much as her pupils did. She stared at the big clock which hung on the wall of the classroom every two minutes. The thought that she would soon be with him was enough to make her giddy.

"Miss, your sums are incorrect," Susan, the smartest pupil in the class, piped up, halting Seara's thought and bringing her back into the class. Seara looked at the answers she had made on the board and saw that they were truly incorrect.

She thanked Susan and apologized to the class of students who giggled softly behind their palms, happy to see that their teacher could also make mistakes.

"That's enough now, kids" She chided them softly, and the giggles stopped abruptly.

"Now, let's open page three of our textbooks, kids...do exercise four as your assignment. It is to be submitted first thing on Monday morning, please, no excuses." She informed.

"Yes, Miss Seara," the children chorused just as the closing bell rang.

Seara hurriedly arranged her books onto her bookshelf, grabbed her jacket, and packed her bags, smiling at the thought that after a month of not seeing him, she would be wrapped in his arms soon. She took out her phone to check if she had any messages from him, but there were none.

Regardless, she knew his car would be parked just outside the school building, waiting for her.

As she stepped out of the school building, she saw his car parked in the school garage. He was sitting in the driver's seat and was speaking on the phone. Seeing him, she felt a little tickle traveling around her stomach. She half ran, and half walked to the car.

When he saw her coming, he came out of the car and held out his arms. In seconds, she was in his arms, weeping softly. The students stared, whistled, and giggled. Seara did not mind. She didn't care about anything when she was in his arms.

"Hey kids, what's good?" he waved to the kids, and the students laughed happily and waved back. He was just that person, personable and friendly. He was also very virile and sexy.

"Hey miss, how was your day?" he asked, running his fingers gently over her hair while looking into her eyes.

"I've missed you, Mac," she smiled, placing her head on his chest.

"I know, babe; I missed you too." He guided her to the other side of the car, opened the door, and settled her lovingly on the seat. Then he came into the driver's seat. Finally, alone in the car, he grabbed her around the waist and brushed his lips against hers. She moaned as pleasure coursed through her.

"Welcome back! It's so good to see you," she said when they disengaged. He started the car and drove casually out of the school premises. She stared at his side profile as he drove.

He caught her staring and smiled at her. She saw longing in his eyes...and something else. A touch of sadness was in his eyes, which made Seara very worried.

Was he sick? Did something terrible happen at his job? she wondered. She wouldn't ask him yet. It was evident that he wasn't ready to tell her whatever the problem was, and she herself was reluctant to spoil the happy mood she was in.

They talked about other things instead. Happy things. She told him about her students and regaled him with funny stories of them. He told her about his job.

Mac, short for Malcolm, was a volunteer for about ten non-governmental organizations, or NGOs as he called them. He was a humanitarian aid and had his own NGO, which catered for the homeless and helpless kids. Mac was very passionate about his work; his passion for helping people was one of the things she loved about him, and it was what had brought them together.

They had met a year ago while he was overseeing a new NGO for young, homeless boys that had just been established. Seara had been sent by her boss to get two of the children so they could be enrolled in school. Sears worked for a private Montessori school with a high price tag for tuition. Her school often did this every new session. The board of the school believed it was a way to give back to the community.

Seara had gotten to the building where the NGO had been situated and met Mac, surrounded by dirty, homeless kids. He was playing a game of chess with them, and he would often allow them to win.

The children cracked smiles they had forgotten they had, and Seara had watched him, fascinated and deeply attracted. She quickly ran to the ladies and fixed her hair, letting some strands fall over her face in a sexy way, and also retouched the little makeup she wore. She had adjusted her skirt and let it ride over her knee to look more sexy for him before going back to meet him.

He was still playing with the children when she came back. When he failed to notice her, she cleared her throat loudly.

He lifted his head and fixed his dreamy grey eyes and dimpled smile on her. After that moment, her life had changed, never to be the same again.

"Hello. Can I help you?"

"Yes...um, no...I mean, yes," she stammered, terribly nervous, "I came for the boys."

"Oh, you are the teacher? Miss Seara?" She loved the way he said her name. He stressed the 'S' quite well.

"Yes, I am," she said, returning his smile.

"I am Mac; I'm currently supervising the project...do you have a specific child in mind?"

"No, I would leave that to your discretion." She put an escaped braid of rich auburn hair behind her ears nervously.

He then gave her two gangly boys and told her not to bother bringing them back. He would come pick them up himself when they were done. Back at the school, Seara anticipated his arrival with a trembling heart. She was in love, and there was no cure for it.

When he came back for the boys, she was ready for him. She made sure the boys sat in her classroom so she would see him again.

"Hello miss," he said as he came in.

"Oh no, please call me Seara," she smiled up at him from her seat.

"Seara." It slipped off his lips like he was tasting it. "You can just call me Mac."

"Okay...Mac, will you bring them yourself tomorrow?" He was silent for a while, staring at her. "Yes, if you want," he said slowly, suddenly avoiding her gaze.

She smiled, "Yes, I would like it if you brought them every day." His laughter rang all over the room, and Seara watched, fascinated by him.

"Will you...um...will you go to dinner with me, Seara?" he had asked.

He took her to a Thai restaurant and apologized for not taking her to a more sophisticated place, as his job as a humanitarian aid didn't pay much. He was relatively broke, to say the least. He still promised that she would enjoy the food regardless.

She had to assure him that she was perfectly fine with the place. The evening was one she would never forget. He had been the perfect gentleman. She had asked why he worked as a humanitarian aid, and he had looked so sad, making her regret the question. But then, he started talking. He told her the saddest tale she had ever heard.

When he was young, about sixteen years old, he was on the basketball team, one of the jocks, and a totally cool kid. He pulled girls easily and had many friends. One of his friends had a mean streak in him and was quickly identified as a bully. He bullied weaker students for fun, and they would all laugh with him when he did. He usually bullied a particular boy the most. This boy came from a very dysfunctional home. He was usually beaten by his drug-addict foster father and sexually assaulted by his foster mother. He was a total loser and had no friends in school, so he was the perfect victim of bullies.

Mac's friend had found out about the boy's home situation and told everyone, which made the boy a laughingstock. The boy then confronted Mac's friend in the dressing room full of the whole team of basketball players. Mac's friend had then encouraged him to end his sorry life, and everyone laughed. Mac said he hadn't laughed, but he didn't stand up for the poor boy either.

The next day, they were told that the poor boy had committed suicide. Guilt stricken, Mac quit basketball and had been trying to atone for a sin he never committed since then.

Seara tried to make him see that it wasn't his fault, but he would not listen. The evening had ended with them in bed, and since then, they have been together. Occasionally, Mac would travel out of New York for volunteer services for a short period, but it only made their love stronger and their meetings more arduous. Mac, pulling his keys out of the ignition, jolted Seara back to the present. The drive had ended as he parked in the garage of his one-bedroom apartment. He came to open the door for her, and she stepped out of the car.

She took in the familiar setting of his house and flushed with happiness. The decor of the sitting room was masculine. It looked like something other than a space that was lived in, which was understandable since Mac hardly stayed at home.

Mac drew her into his embrace. "I've missed you baby."

Seara wanted him to take her there and then, as she felt her walls pulsating with need for him. She tilted her face up to him for a kiss, and he obliged, kissing her hard.

She lost every rational thought then, On fire as she peeled off her shoes frantically.

"Stop; I want to remove that sexy dress from that incredibly sexy body myself," he whispered in her ear.

"Okay, Mac, I'm all yours." She wrapped her arms around his neck in anticipation.

He carried her to the bedroom and laid her down on the bed. Quickly, he slipped the straps of her gown down her shoulders, and she gasped with desire. The dress slithered down her body, and she was left naked. He smiled beautifully and stared at her full and high breasts. He rubbed her small pink nipples begging to be sucked with his fingers, whispering, "You are the most beautiful woman I've ever seen, Seara...and...and I love you so much," he choked, eyes glinting sadly.

Alarmed, Seara rose on her elbows. "Mac, is something wrong?"

He shook his head and smiled. "Nothing, darling... I'm just happy to be with you right now."

Seara smiled and kissed his calloused palms. He quickly removed his clothes and joined her on the bed, bent down, and kissed her hard while covering her breast with his hand, caressing it with a rhythmic squeeze. She growled softly, and his breath came faster as he slid his fingers into her hot, wet mound teasingly. She moaned, stabbed by desire.

"Do you like that baby?" he asked her, wanting to hear her silky voice before he entered her.

"Oh my god, Mac, I want you inside me now," she groaned.

He kissed her nipples and lifted himself up so that he lay over her beautiful body, making sure that he didn't put his entire weight on her. He entered her, slowly at first, then when her pulsating walls filled the whole length of him, he thrust deeply with hard, rapid strokes. She moaned loudly, lost in her desire; he held back his need in favor of hers, gauging her sighs, fast breathing, and moans. He got blinded by his desire for her and wanted release so badly, but he wanted her release first. Soon, she gasped, moaning as her climax hit. She reached up with her arms and drew his neck downwards, biting softly at his lips.

Seara dozed off after their lovemaking and woke up to him staring down at her face with sad eyes. She sat upright and stared at him suspiciously. "Okay, Mac, spit it out," she said to him, afraid of what she was about to hear.

"Spit what out?" he asked, stalling for time.

"Don't be deliberately obtuse with me, Mac; you know what I am talking about. You have been sad since we met earlier. You have something to tell me, so spit it out," she ordered, getting up from the bed.

Mac stretched his arm and gently pulled her down next to him. "Sit babe, please."

She snuggled up to him. "Tell me, I can take it," she pleaded with him.

"I'm going to Africa, Seara," he blurted out, burying his face in his palms. Seara stared at him for a long while, not comprehending what he was saying.

"Did you hear me, babe? I am going to Africa," he repeated.

She sat, without moving at all, shocked to her bone.

"Africa? For what?" she asked very softly, her voice almost inaudible.

"I have volunteered to help with refugees in a small town in Rwanda," he said weakly.

She stood up suddenly. "You intend to leave me to go to a village in Africa? Are you serious, Mac?" she asked, hands shaking with rage and pain.

"Seara, I had no choice. Nobody else was willing to go-"

"Of course, nobody else volunteered to go. It is a horrible idea, that's why, but you just had to play savior again, didn't you?" She interjected furiously.

"That's not fair, Seara," He protested weakly.

"No, don't tell me what is not fair, Mac. What is not fair is you not caring about us enough to control yourself from volunteering for something that will obviously cost you your relationship," She shouted, hyperventilating.

Mac stood up and hugged her tightly, and she struggled to break away from his embrace. She soon got tired and sobbed in his arms. She hit his chest, trying to inflict her pain on him.

"I care about us, Seara, I swear I do, but those people....they need me...If you only saw how helpless they looked," He tried to persuade her.

"No, I don't care if they need you, I do not care how helpless they looked...all I care about is that they will have you, and I won't." She sobbed.

"I'm sorry, babe... I'm so sorry," he said into her hair that smelled of the lavender oil he had bought for her two months ago. She quietened down, and Mac led her to the bed. They sat in silence, each thinking of what they would do without the other.

"You know, that boy's death is not your cross to bear," Seara broke the silence.

Mac shook his head. "It's not because of that, Seara."

"We both know that is why, Mac...I know you are still haunted by his death, and your guilt is pushing you to be a martyr.... but you can never save everyone; no matter what you do, there will still be people who won't get any help. That is how the world is, Mac. If you are going to ever be happy, you must choose to not carry that guilt." Seara said, taking his hands in hers. He averted his face and turned it to the wall. Seara felt her heart break into pieces. He would never change his mind. He was determined to go, she could see. She dropped his hands and frankly asked when he would be going.

"Sunday," he blurted, looking everywhere but her direction.

She made a strangled sob. "I see you are eager to leave so soon."

"I'm sorry... please, Seara; I promise I will find a way to come back early."

Seara knew this was the end of their relationship. He would never come back. He would go from one volunteer job to the other until he probably dropped dead. It was wishful thinking to think he would come back to her. She decided that there was nothing else she could do to stop him. She told him that she knew he would not come back to her; he denied it, but Seara knew she was right.

"Would you spend the remaining days with me before we say goodbye?" He asked sadly, and Seara nodded. They spent the rest of the day making love and taking walks. They cried together when they recollected the beautiful times they spent together and laughed with abandon. On their last night together, Mac took her to the Thai restaurant where they had gone for their first date. As they sat down, Mac reminded her of the night they had spent there, and Seara smiled sadly at the memories.

"Do you think that woman later divorced her husband?" She asked, referring to the woman who had caught her husband having dinner with another woman and had caused a scene that night.

"Hmmm," Mac pretended to think seriously about the question, "No, I don't think so. She would have been too chicken to do so after her husband had pleaded with her and bought her enough jewelry." He joked, and Seara laughed. It was a night filled with bittersweet memories for them. When they got back home, they made love and cried in each other's arms.

The next day, Seara refused to follow him to the airport, fearing that she would run after him onto the plane, cling to him, and then embarrass both herself and him.

She helped him pack, and he gave her the keys to his apartment. She promised to clear out the place for him and send whatever item he might need. They flagged down a taxi together.

Mac stared very long at her, trying to commit her to memory while Seara sobbed softly. "I love you Seara, and I will miss you. Goodbye," he said and kissed her fiercely. Then he entered the cab, and he was gone.

She sobbed softly as she walked home. Saying goodbye indeed hits different when you are with your favorite person in the world, she thought.

CHAPTER SIX

It Hits Different When It's Not What You Expected!

New York never slept. Its heartbeat pulsed with the rhythm of bustling streets, sirens wailing in the distance, and the hushed conversations of secrets exchanged in shadowy alleys.

Neon lights cast eerie colors on rain-slicked pavements, and Dofi stood beneath a flickering streetlight, clutching a weathered envelope, pretty face etched with anticipation and a touch of trepidation. Dofi didn't even know the contents of the envelope, but she knew it definitely wouldn't end well.

When her brother, Trenton Williams, had placed a call to her from the penitentiary yesterday, she didn't want to pick up. God knows she didn't even want to call him by the name Trenton—The white-washed name that he picked up here in America. His name was Kani, and that very name was her first word as she wobbled on unsteady legs through moving boxes as a baby. Kani was a twin, but the name of the other, Kofi, was etched on a grave somewhere behind a church in Harlem. You win some, you lose some.

Dofi sometimes wondered if it all happened because she never called his name.

Their immigrant parents never spoke of the son they lost after moving to The White Man's land. But that never mattered to Dofi and Kani; they were New Yorkians through and through. By the age of eighteen, Kani had adapted to the streets quickly and had a rap sheet longer than Dofi's yaki extensions. He always returned in a cloud of smoke and a suspicious white tint around his nose.

Dofi stepped out of the streetlight's glow and retreated into the darkness once again. Kani had given explicit instructions. "Do, please take the envelope in my room and take it to the Lower East Side in Manhattan. Right next to the old church and hand it to the guy." His words were hushed and eerie as he spoke, breathing loudly through the speakers.

One thing about Kani was his ability to pull people in. That's probably why he became a D boy. It was fast money and needed nothing more than his muscular build and dimpled smile. A big fuck you to their dad, who wanted his son to become a lawyer. You win some, you lose some.

Dofi's dad didn't win any in this situation. His only daughter went on to get pregnant at the age of seventeen. Now that she was twenty one, unemployed, and struggling to feed her five year old, Tricia. Kani called her a hypocrite for naming her child Tricia, but it was better than her getting bullied at the lunch table. The screeching sound of a Ford Mustang coming to a halt drew Dofi out of her thoughts, and her muscles pulled tense. "Trenton?" A gruff voice asked from the car, barely visible in the dim lighting of the street.

Dofi hesitated in the shadows and nervously picked at the edges of her ripped jeans. She knew there was a high chance that the box in her hands contained dope, crack, or even meth. Every single brain cell in her head screamed loudly at her to turn around, to run away. But before she could even make up her mind. The voice sounded again. "It's dark there, but it ain't that dark. We can see you come on out."

"Give me a second," Dofi muttered, inching out of the darkness. The sentence for drug trafficking was about three years for a first time offender. Tricia would be eight, going on to nine before she got out, and her brows furrowed into a tight line. She really hadn't thought this through.

A tall man stepped out as Dofi walked up to the car. His chocolate skin was adorned with tattoos on every visible space, and Dofi felt jealous, trying to catch a glimpse of his face.

The darkness and his baseball cap did her no favors, hiding every part of his face. "You're not Trenton. Never mind, just get into the car," The tattooed man ordered, holding the passenger door wide open.

"I'm just a delivery guy. Here's the box, I brought it with me." Dofi felt her heart thud harshly against her chest. Following him to God knows where wasn't part of the plan. She hurriedly shoved the box into the man's chest and prepared to run off into the cold night. The man grabbed the box, and Dofi, with a singular motion, pushed her into the car.

As the man pushed Dofi into his Ford Mustang, the leather seats were surprisingly cold against her skin. She held tightly onto the box, fingers turning white from all the force. She couldn't help but mutter the Lord's Prayer despite being an avowed atheist. "The father who is up in heaven…" She couldn't help but chuckle inwardly at the irony of her plea.

Her fingers anxiously traced the edges of the box as she wondered what she had gotten herself into.

The tattooed man navigated the darkened streets of New York City with an air of confidence. The city lights streaked past, casting eerie shadows in the car's interior. Dofi felt her heart racing as she tried to make sense of the situation. She still couldn't see the man's face clearly, hidden under his baseball cap, but his strong presence filled the car.

Eventually, the car came to a halt in front of a neon-lit club. Von turned to Dofi, his voice firm, "Get out."

"No." Dofi hesitated, glancing at the club's entrance. It was a place far removed from the life of a mother with a five-year-old daughter who had picture day at school the next morning. She clung to the box, her fingers unwilling to let go.

But Von was unrelenting. "I ain't got time for this fucking bullshit." He got out, walked over, grabbed her arm, and forcefully pulled her out of the car. Dofi stumbled, but her grip on the box remained unwavering.

With Von's arm still tight around hers, he led her toward the club's entrance. There, a burly bouncer stood guard, dapping the tattooed guy up as he reached the door. "Yo, Von."

Von. Her captor's name was Von.

"Johnny, what's up." Von greeted, exposing his face to the neon lights that lit up the entrance.

Dofi looked up at his face, tracing his rugged features and the scar that ran across his left cheek. He looked like Kani. At that point, every troubled young man looked like Kani to Dofi. Was it the scars? Was it the rugged determination to keep going down the rabbit hole of darkness? She honestly didn't know, and she might never know with the night still hanging in the balance.

"Is the boss in?" Von questioned, jaw clenched. Johnny had his arms crossed in the classic burly bouncer style.

"Yes, he came in with Deshawn just an hour ago."

They exchanged hushed words, and Dofi gathered that Von was a familiar figure here. Von confirmed Johnny's acknowledgment with a friendly dap before returning his attention to Dofi. "Move."

Avoiding eye contact, Dofi followed Von through the pulsating neon lights and writhing bodies of clubgoers into a dimly lit hallway off to the side. It stretched out before them, and at the end, two doors awaited. Peeking into the left room, she spotted another hallway, but Von guided her to the first door on the right.

The room they entered was an empty office devoid of any other occupants. Von wasted no time and unceremoniously threw Dofi into a black leather chair. "Don't move a single muscle."

He stepped out, locking the door behind him, leaving Dofi alone in the dimly lit room.

As her eyes adjusted to the surroundings, she couldn't help but take a closer look. The gloomy office had an air of authority about it, with dark wooden furniture and a leather-bound chair behind a heavy oak desk. On the desk, a few papers lay scattered, and a desk lamp cast a soft, warm glow.

"Curiosity killed the cat. Curiosity killed the goddamned cat." Dofi chanted, trying to keep her curiosity in check. But fear and desperation fueled her curiosity.

Dofi started searching for any clues about the 'boss' she was supposed to deliver the box to or about her brother's involvement in all of this. She scanned the room for pictures, certificates, or any mementos that might provide answers. But the office had no hint of personal touches, offering no insights into the identity of its occupant.

Her eyes then fell upon a cabinet tucked away in the corner. The carvings on its surface matched those on the box her brother had asked her to deliver.

Determination overcame caution as she approached the cabinet, prying it open with trembling hands.

Inside, she discovered two files neatly organized and a set of large, ornate rings. Her heart pounded in her chest as she searched through the files, hoping for a clue. Yet, despite her efforts, the files revealed nothing substantial.

Just as she was about to give up, heavy sounds of footsteps reached her ears, along with the muffled boom of club music. Von was about to come in; she looked at the scattered cabinet and cussed loudly.

"Fuck."

The door creaked open, and Von spoke, locking the door behind him again, his voice a low rumble, "Give me the box."

Dofi hid her trembling hands under the box that was now back in her lap. Her brown eyes darted to the file sticking out of the ornate cabinet, and her heart pounded wildly.

"Oh, fine." She reluctantly handed over the box, but before she could breathe a sigh of relief, Von asked for something unexpected, "The key."

"What key?" Confusion washed over her. She had assumed the key would be with the intended recipient of the box, not her. Dofi's mind raced as she tried to make sense of the situation.

Von's patience seemed to wane as he towered over her, his tattooed arms crossed.

"I don't have it," Dofi finally stammered, her voice quivering with anxiety. The implications of not having the key were unknown to her, but it was clear that Von expected her to have it.

Von let out an exasperated sigh, his piercing gaze locked onto Dofi's. "You were supposed to have it. Trenton wouldn't have entrusted you with this if he didn't think you could handle it."

The mention of her brother's name sent a shiver down Dofi's spine. She knew that Kani had his secrets and had likely kept her in the dark about many things. But now, she was caught in a situation that seemed to grow more complex by the minute. Kani went to jail last month for possession, just a few weeks after he swore he had gotten clean.

Their parents cut him off, and she did, too. Even the call was a shock. How was she supposed to know about the key?

Dofi's confusion was palpable as she fumbled to understand what Von meant by "the key." She had never been informed of any key accompanying the box.

Von leaned in closer, his dark eyes locked onto hers. "You know what I'm talking about," he hissed, his voice laced with a hint of danger.

Dofi's mind raced, desperately trying to recall any additional instructions her brother might have given her. But as she searched her memory, she drew a blank. She had been focused solely on the box, never expecting there would be a key involved.

"I really don't have a key," she stammered, her anxiety mounting with each passing second. She wished she had asked more questions and demanded more answers from her brother.

Von's eyes bore into her, and for a moment, it felt as though he could see right through her. "Think, girl. Think hard."

Dofi's heart raced, and she racked her brain for any possible clue. She remembered the cabinet in the corner of the office, its carvings matching those on the box. Could there be a connection? She hesitated for a moment, then blurted out, "There's a cabinet in the corner, like the one on the box. Maybe... maybe the key is in there?"

Von's expression didn't change, but he nodded as though he had expected this revelation. "Show me."

Dofi reluctantly led him to the cabinet, heart pounding louder than the club music echoing through the walls. She pointed to the ornate carvings, her fingers trembling as she tried to open the cabinet once more. As the cabinet door swung open, a sense of trepidation hung in the air. Inside, they found a collection of files and the same set of large, intricate rings. But there, nestled beneath the folders, was a small key, its metal glinting faintly in the soft office lighting.

Von reached for the key, his tattooed fingers closing around it.

Dofi experienced a blend of emotions, a mixture of relief and anxiety. The key appeared to be the crucial element missing from the puzzle. However, it also meant she was becoming more deeply involved in a complex network of concealed matters she couldn't entirely grasp.

"Now," Von declared, his voice hushed and authoritative, "you will remain here. I have matters to address, and you won't be allowed to leave until I return."

He exited the room, locking the door, and Dofi found herself in solitude once more, her thoughts racing with uncertainties and inquiries. What was inside the goddamned box? And where was her brother, Kani, in this freaking scenario?

In the poorly illuminated office, Dofi could do nothing but wait, her heart burdened by the enigma before her. After a few more minutes, Von showed up with the box and handed it to her. "That's not the key. Where is the key? As a matter of fact, where the fuck is Trenton? Boss needs the contents of that box now!"

Dofi's heart sank as she realized that Kani's acquaintances were unaware of his arrest. She couldn't bear the thought of telling them, not when she had no idea what they might do to her if they couldn't reach Trenton.

Von's insistence on finding "Boss" piqued Dofi's curiosity, but she was also growing weary of this harrowing journey. She knew she had to end this nightmarish adventure as soon as possible. She finally made a decision and promised Von, "I can take you to Trenton. Just... let's get this over with."

"Fine, let's get moving," Von agreed, and they walked out, the box still in her arms.

As they made their way through the club once more, Dofi's gaze flickered to the opposite hallway. In the dimly lit corridor, Dofi's eyes met those of a little girl in the arms of a muscular man, surrounded by men in suits who looked like bodyguards.

They walked through the loud club again and stepped out into the chilly night air. Dofi's heart pounded with a mixture of fear and determination. She glanced at Von, unsure of how to proceed, and then, in a moment of nervous hesitation, she blurted out an address.

"Trenton is in Harlem. 54, West Street."

This was the location of the church in Harlem where her other brother, Kofi, was buried. Technically, they were looking for her brother, and she was leading Von to one of them.

It wasn't the entire truth, but in her mind, Kani was her brother, and Kofi, resting in that cemetery, was also her brother. Von drove off with Dofi sitting in the passenger seat, the mysterious box now resting beside her.

During the drive, Von broke the silence, his voice tinged with curiosity. "So, how did you end up doing deliveries for Trenton?" he asked, clearly expecting a straightforward answer.

Dofi, however, was not willing to reveal the family connection. She brushed off the question with a vague response, "Just needed some extra cash, you know?" The less she revealed, the better. She was determined to keep her true identity hidden until she was sure that neither Von nor "Boss" could trace her.

Their journey came to a halt as Von parked the Ford Mustang in front of the church. He scanned the area, his patience waning, and questioned, "This is a church. Where's Trenton?"

Dofi looked around, feigning uncertainty. "I thought he was supposed to deal here earlier tonight." She slowly got out of the car, the box clutched in her arms as if she was merely curious about the surroundings. She stepped closer to the church, scanning for a familiar alley that she had spotted earlier.

In a moment of desperation, she shouted, "Trenton!" while pointing to the opposite side of the road. Von instinctively looked in the direction she pointed, and that's when Dofi seized her chance. She sprinted away, disappearing into the darkened alley as if it were her sanctuary.

Von, infuriated by her escape, slammed his hand on the hood of the car, cursing under his breath. He turned and ran in the opposite direction, determined to find her.

Dofi, hidden in the alley, had a moment to catch her breath. She clutched the box to her chest, heart pounding wildly as she prayed for her escape to go unnoticed. "I swear, I'll be good. I'll look for a job every day, and I'll stop being a bum. Our father…"

But just as she started to calm down, she heard the distinct sound of footsteps approaching in the alley. "Dear God, Holy Mary." Her breath caught in her chest, and she silently uttered another prayer, praying for divine intervention. Von was closing in.

However, before he could discover her hiding place, Von's phone rang. Dofi strained to listen and could make out snippets of the conversation. "Boss…No. I lost the girl and the box." The person on the other end seemed to have instructed him to return to the club immediately.

"Fuck!" Von stamped his foot in frustration but ultimately obeyed the command. Dofi breathed a sigh of relief as she heard the sound of his tires screeching away.

She was safe, for now.

With trembling hands, Dofi returned to her parents' home, being careful not to wake them. She climbed the stairs, her heart heavy with the night's events. She entered her daughter Tricia's room, planting a gentle kiss on her forehead and smoothing out the plastic curlers in her hair. Her pretty white shirt and green plaid skirt sat neatly ironed on the bed next to her. It was picture day today.

Her next destination was Kani's room. Dofi approached his wide mahogany desk, the very spot where she had retrieved the box earlier. There, sitting on the table right next to where she had taken the box, was a key. Her eyes widened as she realized her oversight.

There was a key!
Dofi was torn. She could try to return the key and the box to Von now. But the risk was too high, and her curiosity was too intense to resist any longer. She decided to open the box. If it contained something illegal, she'd have to take her chances with the police, perhaps claiming she found it on the road.

"Kani, I swear to God. I'm not going to jail like you," She muttered an exasperated complaint about her brother's secrets and, with trembling hands, she opened the box. It was lined with soft red velvet, a stark contrast to the uncertainty that had gripped her all night. As she fully opened the box, she was left in stunned disbelief.

Inside, nestled in the plush velvet, were three delicate Chinese glass figurines, each one a work of intricate artistry. Dofi's eyes widened, her breath catching as she stared at them. A white note peeked out from the corner, and she unfolded it, reading it out loud. "Happy fifth birthday, Boss."

She slammed the box shut, collapsing onto Kani's messy bed. "What the fuck, You've got to be kidding me. All this for a kid?"

It sure hits different when things are not what you expected.

CHAPTER SEVEN

It Hits Different When You Make A Bad Choice At The Wrong Time!

The streets of Chicago felt cold, dull, and withered away. Devon, seated on the steps, could smell Joe's presence lingering everywhere. His snorted laughs that sounded like that of a dog and even how he pronounced his name. Devon. Quite the simple one, but Joe had a way of making it look like a Herculean task.

"Hey, Devon! Momma wants you." Khia, his little sister, called out, but he never heard her.

He was still lost in his thoughts. "Devon!" She shouted, stomping her foot down angrily. "Get off your ass and go answer Momma. I'm not leaving my phone for the second time just to call you out of your little mood!" She slammed the door, and off she went. Little Khia could never truly understand Devon's dilemma. Little indeed. Devon was only two years older than her, but that's precisely what she was.

Devon wasn't shocked, though; he was familiar with her bratty behavior. The little eighteen year old that was pampered like an egg, a luxury treatment that he never got to receive as the first child. Slowly, he stood up like a slug, unwilling to move.

Momma wanted Devon to drive her to work. She always did this! She had her own car and license but never wanted to drive. She says she has two grown kids, so she shouldn't have to drive or pay for no Uber. He was about to get in his car when the loud wailing of a police car called his attention, and he paused in his tracks as the car stopped right in front of his house. The sirens wailed louder than he had ever heard, probably because it had never been his house.

He stopped his heart racing and eyes bulging out. He could hear his heart beat loudly, and the guilt all over his face couldn't be hidden.

"Popo? Who are they here for? My money's on Gary from 108, wanna bet?" Khia fired all her thoughts, questions, and assumptions all at once without missing a beat.

"You would lose that bet. They are here for me; I've done a lot wrong," Devon whispered slowly, not noticing his mom, Anita, who had dashed out of the house with her office pants hanging loosely around her waist.

"Devon ain't making no sense. Why are they here, Momma?" Khia asked curiously.

"They're here for me," Devon murmured again. His mom quickly turned in his direction. His words were like a dagger cutting through her heart. Devon knew his dad had gone to jail and died there because of his rugged life. Seeing her son following his dad's footsteps could end his Momma's life immediately.

"What do you mean? What did you do? Devon!" Anita shouted, holding his shirt in a very tight grip as one of the policemen headed towards them,
"Hello, ma'am, we are here to…" the policeman was cut off by Anita. "You can't be here, sir. My son is innocent; you can't take him and kill him like his dad. Not him, never!" she shouted, shielding Devon with her chubby body.
"Quickly, get in the house," she commanded Devon furiously with tears rushing down her cheeks, but he stood still. His legs were frozen. His mouth shut as if glued, and tears rolled down chocolate cheeks. All he could do was stare at his mom, wondering how she was feeling and to what extent.
He knew he had brought hurt and pain to his family, just like his dad.
"Get your ass in here," Anita shouted, pushing him in, but his legs were still fixed to the ground. Just then, he took her hands off his shirt, walked toward the police, and stood still, offering himself to them.

"Take me, I'm guilty!" Devon yelled, raising his hands above his head. Anita was already on her knees. Her tears had stopped flowing now. The moment she feared for so long was happening right in front of her. Devon always loved his father, followed him mostly, and said yes to his wrongs. It has been two years since his father died in prison, dying from a heart attack. Devon's dad was the ringleader of one of the hood's largest gangs. He was deadly, feared, and embodiment of a thug nigga.

Anita has always envisioned her son turning out to be like his dad, and her prayer was for it never to happen. But it did. She has failed.

"You're Mr Devon Deveil?" Asked one of the policemen with a dimple on his left cheek.

"Yes, I am," Devon replied, still hanging his hands, waiting for a cuff to be put over them. "We are here to take you in for questioning. This is not an arrest; kindly get in, Mr. Deveil." The policeman opened the door, and Devon slid in.

Khia was pulling at his shirt as if he was about to be killed. "Let go Khia." He removed her hands gently, and the policeman shut the door.

The police car drove off, and Devon peeped through the back window of the vehicle. He saw his mom wailing as if her tears were hidden just until he got into the car. As for Khia, she was on the floor next to their mom. Tears rolled down his cheeks as he steeled his resolve.

Soon, Devon was at the door of the police station. It was a quick ride, indeed. Quicker than he had expected for a police station that seemed miles away from him before. Devon thought, "They ass don't show up that quick when you need them."

He remembered slamming these exact doors when his dad was there before. He had cussed the police out, calling them the same names his dad had affectionately dubbed them. "Bitch ass niggas" and "Shit of the streets."

His father, Donny, would mumble that anytime he came close to any station. Devon never saw wrongs in his father, and so he hated the police and called them fake ass bitches.

He walked the path his father walked and found himself seated in the same seat his dad had probably sat on. He was about to be questioned by a white man; his badge read his name. Charles.

"You are Mr. Devon Deveil?" Charles asked.

"I am," Devon replied, head bent. His hands began to shake, forcing him to hide them under the table immediately. Cold sweat dripped down his face onto his worn jeans, leaving dark, wet spots.

"Calm down, as we'll just be asking some simple questions." Charles tried to calm him down. He probably noticed how tense and scared Devon was. But before Charles could continue, gunshots were heard outside of the police station.

"You, stay with Devon!" Charles shouted as he rushed out of the interrogation room.

Devon opened his eyes. He was confused and scared. He was still a kid, just 20, and was willing to admit that he had done wrong. He remembered how he had pulled the cold metal trigger, pointing the nuzzle at his friend, Joe. They were once friends, but their paths in the streets had separated them.

Devon had no idea how it all happened. But he was determined to have revenge on a story he knew barely anything about. He had joined one of the neighborhood sets, the Fairfield Crips.

Joe, on the other hand, claimed Wolcott, a Blood gang in the hood a few blocks over. He joined them to protect himself. Joe was the total opposite of Devon. He wore large glasses that belonged on the face of an old man, and his slight frame added no points when it came to bullies at school. He never wanted to be in that situation they were in the night before, and he had absolutely no explanations or proof of Devon's accusations. The Wolcott and Fairfield were both younger sets that had not been around that long, but they had beef.

No one was sure how it started, and Devon was pretty sure that nobody wanted to.

One Sunday night, Fairfield had planned to pull up on Wolcott. His boys had triggered him, cussed him out, and called him a "pussy" and a lil Bitch," putting a gun on his hand and making plans for him. He was on the edge of being jumped out and losing his life, so yes, he obliged them.

The plans they had were executed perfectly, and Joe was the first to fall victim. His boys scattered immediately; Fairfield had them cornered. Joe lost his glasses in the clash and could barely see his nose. Guns were brandished carelessly, and none of them expected what came next.

With a bang, Joe was shot, and the gun was in Devon's hand. Devon could swear he never remembered pulling the trigger, but he was the only one with the single gun that Fairfield had. There was no backup gun, as it was hard for young black gang groups to acquire guns. Everyone knew and feared what they would do with it.

The blood on the floor that Sunday night flooded the curb, and it was all Joe's blood. Devon had pulled the trigger just as a black SUV car passed by, brushing right past him with a loud screeching sound. More gunshots were heard, and both gangs fled, leaving Joe to his fate.

Devon had uttered no words. He crept into his home and had gone days without food or coming outside. He thought he had ended his friend's life, and today proved it all right. The police had brought him here to make him pay.

And he was willing to pay.

Devon was still lost in thoughts when he heard the slamming of the doors and shouts, "Move them in," Charles ordered.

Another gang called Wood Street Crips was caught trying to retrieve their leader from the hands of the police. The Wood Street had intended to break their leader, Dante', out of cell tonight. There were 15 members, and all were moved to different compartments for their statements. They had sustained severe gunshot injuries.

"Mr. Devon, you wait here, and I'll be back for you in an hour," Charles said before walking into one of the compartments, after which screams were heard.

After Wood Street had dropped their statements, Charles came out. Three hours had gone by, and Devon was seated with his mom. The police department had permitted them after being asked to do so by Mr Charles following the evidence, statement, and report he had gotten from the Wood Street group. Devon wept into his mother's arms. "I've made a big mistake. What have I done, Momma? I wish I could take it back and do it all over. Would he ever forgive me!" he yelled.

Charles hurriedly intervened. "You did nothing except mingling with the wrong crowd. "Joe was shot, but it was a stray. Wood Street had a drive-by on an opposing gang member who was a blood hanging out with Wolcott. None of you were the target, but wrong place, wrong time."

Charles reached into a drawer and brought out some papers. "Here," he passed them to Devon and his mom.

"This is a picture of a black SUV involved in the incident. The bullet extracted from Joe's body is registered under Dante', one of the gang leaders."

Devon was shocked and startled. He stood up from his seat with his hands shaking. He had deemed his memory faulty for not remembering the shooting. He doubted himself and took all the blame. But he was right initially; he never took the shot because he couldn't.

"He is still gone!" he mumbled.

Devon immediately began to sob. It hit different when bad choices were made at the wrong time.

CHAPTER EIGHT

Hoodies Hit Different When It's Not Yours!

It was merely a few days leading up to Mardi Gras, and foreigners flocked to the city with hopes of catching the most exciting time of the year in New Orleans.

You could easily spot them in the crowd with their gleeful eyes, loud laughter, excited cheers, and cameras hanging down their necks. It was obvious in their colorful outfits that grated on Keon's eyes as he walked down the street toward his best friend's bar.

Each of the Mardi Gras fans usually got what they came down here for, as Mardi Gras succeeded in living up to its name each year. The streets were rich in color with bands, singers, and drummers, making every rhythm worth their time.

Mardi Gras happens every year, and one would think someone who has lived in New Orleans all their life would have gotten used to it. But the locals down here were always as excited each time like dogs with the same chewed-out bone.

The weeks of celebration and festivals came with so much color that it affected even the most boring person, but Keon couldn't care less about Mardi Gras. This week had been a hectic one, he lost his side gig at the restaurant downtown, and his new boss kept giving him shit. On days like this, he just wanted a stiff bourbon, and as he walked through the French Quarter, he hurried along and avoided bumping into anyone as though he were avoiding the infectious disease that was Mardi Gras.

A group of attractive Mardi Gras revelers dressed in elaborate costumes adorned with sequins and feathers noticed Keon as he passed by. The women in sensual outfits couldn't resist the temptation to interact with this brooding figure amidst their celebration.

One of the women, a vivacious brunette with emerald green eyes, stepped forward and blocked Keon's path. She wore a glittering, form-fitting dress that accentuated her curves. With a captivating smile, she said, "Hey there, handsome. Don't you want to join in on the fun? It's Mardi Gras!"

Keon, his expression still stern, looked down at her with a hint of annoyance in his deep brown eyes. He didn't appreciate the intrusion. "I've got no interest in all this chaos," he replied, his voice steady and unwavering.

Undeterred, another woman, this one with a fiery red wig and a costume that sparkled like a disco ball, joined in. She playfully twirled a strand of her hair and said, "Come on, don't kill the vibe. It's just one day a year!"

"It sounds delightful, but I'll pass." Keon's jaw tightened, and he stepped to the side, bypassing them as he stepped into a bar right at the corner.

Keon knew he was attractive, and the ladies obviously knew it, too, but he just wanted to get his bourbon.

Inside the dimly lit bar, the lively chatter of patrons and the clinking of glasses filled the air. Keon found solace at the worn wooden counter, and he signaled the familiar bartender, a stout man with a thick mustache. "Hey, Slick. My usual."

"Coming right up," he nodded in acknowledgment. "Here you go, bourbon sour just as you like it."

Just as Keon received his drink, a familiar voice called out to him from across the bar. "Kee, my man!"

Keon spun around with a jerk, taking a sip of the sweet and sour goodness in his hands. It was his best friend, Marcus, a tall man with just the right amount of cash to go into an early retirement. "Hey, Marcus."

Marcus waved him over, his own Mardi Gras attire consisting of a colorful feathered mask and a jester's hat.

Keon couldn't help but crack a faint smile at the sight of Marcus. He downed his first glass and requested another before walking over to Marcus at a corner table.

"Kee, I've got a friend with me. Meet Ayesha." Marcus checked his phone impatiently, typing furiously on his screen as he spoke.

That's when Keon saw her.

She sat next to Marcus, a striking figure in a teal hoodie and a full head of black curls. Her caramel-colored skin glowed in the dimly lit bar, and her eyes, the color of dark coffee, sparkled with warmth and intelligence. With a friendly smile, she extended her hand towards Keon, exuding confidence that drew him in. "Hello, I'm Ayesha."

"I'm key…Keon, I mean. You can just call me key yunno," Kean stumbled over his words, rubbing nonexistent dust off the corner of his shirt cuff.

Slick returned with a second glass of bourbon, but the sound of the glass on the hardwood table didn't make Keon peel his eyes away from the woman in front of him.

Marcus jolted Keon out of his state with a loud shout. "Damn, Mark and the guys are out front. Kee, wanna come?"

"Nope," Keon responded with a roll of his eyes. Marcus was his friend, but that didn't make Marcus's white friends his friends by association. He had made the mistake of tagging along for their boys' trip to Greece last month, and things had gotten real wild: drugs, women, lots of booze, you know, some crazy shit.

Keon loved a good time, but it kinda stops being a good time when the cops crash the party and arrest you and then Marcus—the only other black guy in the room. The so-called friends partied on and returned to New Orleans while Marcus's Dad had to send his lawyer to bail Keon and Marcus out.

"Stop giving me that look; it's just a party downtown. Y'all are great company, but I gotta go now. Have fun, Ayesha and you, Key, we gon talk later." Marcus rushed out, his outfit flailing around his muscled frame.

Now that he was alone with Ayesha, Keon couldn't resist. Maybe the buzz from his second glass had something to do with it. His fingers tapped nervously at his glass as he contemplated what to say when the inscription on her teal green hoodie made him laugh.

"Hoodies hit different when they aren't ours," He read out loud right beside her, and she looked up, giving him her full attention again.

She patted her curls down at the side with a ringed hand and gave Keon a naughty smile. "They do be hitting different."

"So I can assume that it's your job. You steal hoodies for a living?" Keon asked, half joking. He was actually curious and wanted to know more about her, and he once dated a girl who was obsessed with his hoodies. Marcus would make fun of him whenever he let her have them.

Ayesha replied with a scoff and a smile at the corner of her mouth. "I'm a lawyer, and stealing hoodies is just my side gig."

"That's great. Are you considering expanding the business or branching out?" Keon replied, matching her pace.

Ayesha quickly grabbed a chair and fished for a pen in her brown duffel bag at the side. "Oh, that would be lovely. I'm sure I have my business card and investment papers in here somewhere."

"Shit," Keon cackled, doubling over the table in laughter. "You really are committed to your business."

"That's how the warmth bills are getting paid." She nodded in agreement, accompanying it with a smile that was enough to melt the jazz out of a gris-gris.

Keon drank her in, enamored even more than he was a second ago. There was just something about her. Her smile, her eyes, her humor. She was perfect. "I've never heard Marcus talk about you before. You from these parts?"

"Nope. I'm from LA. I came down here for the Mardi Gras."

Of all the reasons why she was in New Orleans, it just had to be Mardi Gras. Keon looked out the window at the colorful crowd and back to the casually dressed beauty across the table. "You don't look it."

"That's so judgy. I've got a lot of color in my hoodie. It's a greenish blue kinda." She looked down at her hoodie, running her fingers over the design.

"Teal. It's teal green," Keon corrected. "Also, you look stunning. You're just missing the feathers and sparkles. So you came here alone?"

"Nope, I came with my friends."

Keon watched her face light up as she cheerfully shared how her friends had eagerly planned the trip because they saw The Originals and wanted to feel what it was like to walk the same streets as the great Klaus Mikaelson.

He smiled as an acknowledgment to show that he was listening as she rambled on. It was cute to watch. He was done with the second glass now, and he figured they could walk around the French Quarter for a bit. "Could I delight you in a walk through the great streets?"

He could even take her downtown if she wanted, but a lot of foreigners avoided wandering to those parts as much as possible.

"I thought you'd never ask," she chirped, slinging her bag onto her shoulder. Her glossed lips seemed to be placed in a permanent smile from the moment their hoodie banter had started.

"So, do you steal them?" Keon asked again as he held out the door for her.

"What?"

"What?" Keon asked, confused as they stepped out into the setting sun.

Ayesha paused mid-step, and Keon could have sworn that he saw the wheels turning in her head. "You mean the hoodie? I don't steal hoodies….I take them," She said as she hopped a few steps ahead.

He doubled his pace to catch up with her, and as they kept walking and talking. The festive feeling in the air wrapped tighter around him like a Boy Scout knot. Maybe Mardi Gras wasn't so bad after all. "Would you like to go on the flying horses at the city park? They have it there every year, and people seem to love it."

Ayesha shook her head, a refusal right on the tips of her now parted lips. "Actually, a nice stroll would—"

He grabbed her hand before she could protest and hailed a taxi. "City Park."

It felt like a friendly kidnapping, if that made any sense, and the weird image threw the two of them into fits of laughter in the backseat. The disdainful look from the driver didn't bother Keon as they pulled up to City Park, and he paid, holding onto Ayesha with his free hand.

In the large park that stretched over 1300 acres, Keon and Ayesha found themselves on one of the amusement rides, their fifth merry-go-round of the day. As they disembarked, laughter filled the air, and they clutched their bellies, thoroughly enjoying the whirlwind of joy. Keon turned to Ayesha, his eyes twinkling with delight, and asked, "Isn't this great?"

Ayesha, still catching her breath, nodded vigorously, her hand pressed to the side of her stomach as her laughter echoed. "Absolutely, Keon, this is so much fun!"

With a playful grin, Keon suggested, "How about we head over to Frenchmen Street? It's just outside the French Quarter, and it's a vibrant nightlife district. There's incredible food, drinks, street performers, and even a beautiful art gallery. It's got a little bit of everything."

Excitement filled Keon's voice as he hoped to make a memorable impression on Ayesha. He thought, "Maybe my buddies will see me with this beautiful girl and stop teasing me."

She glanced at her watch, realizing she had commitments with her friends. Determined to make the most of their time, he assured her, "Don't worry, I'll get you back in time. As long as I return before midnight. Let's have some fun first."

As they approached Frenchmen Street, the melodious sounds of a live band reached their ears. A growing crowd had gathered around, swaying to the rhythm of the music. Keon couldn't resist the allure, and he extended his hand towards Ayesha. "Care to dance?"

Ayesha, her eyes sparkling with adventure, accepted his invitation and joined the impromptu dance floor. She mirrored his movements as they swayed to the music, her body effortlessly syncing with his.

The live performance reached its crescendo, filling the air with a crescendo of notes, and the crowd erupted in cheers. As they made their way from the epicenter of music and excitement, Keon gently took Ayesha's hands in his, locking eyes with her. He asked, "I hope you had a good time. Was that okay?"

Ayesha's smile was radiant as she tucked a loose strand of hair behind her ear with her right hand. "More than okay, Keon. It was fantastic."

Keon wanted to kiss her so bad, but it was rushed, right? They had chemistry, but what if she didn't think so? It was complicated, and the sky had darkened, ushering them into the New Orleans nightlife.

"Would you like to chill in my apartment?" Keon winced immediately as those words left his mouth. He sounded like an old geezer trying to lure innocent children into the back of his truck.

"Sure, is it close by?" Ayesha asked, obviously obliging to his request.

Keon stared at her again with a bit of wonder mixed in. "Yeah, it's just right around the corner here. No stranger danger?"

"You're not exactly a stranger anymore, and the danger is right here in my bag," Ayesha grinned, flashing a large Taser from inside her brown bag.

They both laughed again, and they walked down the street, pretending not to notice as their hands brushed gently against each other. Each brush of their skin sent jolts of electricity up Keon's arm, and he felt his cheeks flush. He heaved a sigh of relief as they reached his apartment building. "Ri—right here. Let's go up."

The elevator ride was quiet, the total opposite of their loud conversations since they met in the afternoon. The emotions coursing through them needed silence. A loud ping cut through the maintained silence and resettled as Keon led her to a brown door at the end of the hallway. "Come in."

His bedroom was cozy and had several vinyl records coupled with posters of local musicians.

"Sure." Ayesha obliged, and as the lights came on in his living room, his mouth came crashing down on hers. It was hard, rushed, and full of passion. Their tension and attraction had finally exploded, and even the slightest touch of their skin drove the other into a frenzy. The early hours of the evening faded away under their warm touches.

As they lay underneath the warm sheets, he told her all about his job and his worries. He didn't know why he was being vulnerable, but something about her made him open up. She looked up at him when he was done, and he saw the pity in her eyes as she kissed him deeply right before saying she was sorry about all of it.

It wasn't her place to apologize, but her apology was soothing, a balm to his soul. "Thank you." He tightened his arms around her, basking in her warmth.

"This was amazing, but I've got to go now, Keon," Ayesha whispered, drawing circles on his chest with her ring finger.

"Okay, let me get dressed so I can't walk you back." Keon got out of bed, buttoning his dress shirt in a hurry.

Ayesha also got out of bed, stunning Keon as she walked around his room naked to pick up each item of clothing she had discarded earlier. "I can get a taxi just fine. Don't worry about me."

Keon nodded like a child and sat on the bed, watching her every move. He hated the fact that she couldn't stay the night, but he was in no place to ask for more. "Can I at least have your number?"

"No need for that. If we're meant to see each other again, we will. Don't force things." She placed a kiss on his head and grabbed her bag, looking at him expectantly.

"What?"

"You're supposed to walk me out." Ayesha scolded.

Keon sprang up to his feet and pulled on his shoes. The elevator ride down was as silent as the ride up. He waved her goodbye as the taxi zoomed off, and now, he was just going to sleep into the afternoon, probably. No job, no grumpy boss to yell at him over every little thing.

He twisted his door open and walked back into the apartment that still smelled like Ayesha. She smelt like coffee and vanilla. A teal green hoodie greeted him on the floor next to his bed, and he held it up, hitting his forehead. "Fuck, why didn't I notice that she left it."

The image of her getting into the taxi flashed through his head. She was wearing a plain white baby-tee. The sound of a note falling onto the ground from the hoodie pulled him back to the present and he unfurled it. "Keep it. Hoodies hit different when they aren't yours."

To this day, Ayesha's hoodie is Keon's favorite piece of clothing, and he wears it every Mardi Gras. Making it a point to visit the same bar around the same time, hoping to see Ayesha there again. Since that day, no other Mardi Gras, no other piece of clothing, interaction, or experience has hit quite the same.

CHAPTER NINE

The Truth Hit Different When It's Not What You Wanted

The air inside the police station hung heavy, thick with the scent of stale coffee and nervous sweat. Fluorescent lights flickered overhead, casting flickering shadows across the scuffed linoleum floors. Detective Monique Carter, a no-nonsense woman with a tightly wound bun and a penchant for colorful language, leaned against the front desk, a white Styrofoam cup of lukewarm coffee in hand.

She watched as Jamal, a tall, lanky man with a faded Yankees cap pulled low over his brow, shifted uncomfortably in the worn-out chair. His eyes darted around the room, avoiding eye contact with anyone, especially Detective Anderson, a square-jawed man who gave off an air of authority.

Marcus, on the other hand, sat slouched in his chair, his leather jacket draped over the back, revealing a faded "Brooklyn" tattoo on his forearm. His scuffed boots tapped an impatient rhythm on the linoleum.

Monique couldn't help but notice the beads of sweat forming on their brows, glinting like diamonds under the unforgiving lights. Their faces wore the strain of the long night ahead, and Monique knew she had to tread carefully if she wanted to get to the bottom of this mess.

Another detective who stood behind Monique, Detective Harper, a wiry woman with a steely gaze, took the lead. "Alright, Jamal," she began, her tone firm, "let's go over this again. You said you were at Tony's Bar that night, right?"

Jamal's eyes darted towards her, and he nodded hesitantly. "Yeah, that's right, Detective. I was just having a drink, minding my own business."

Monique couldn't help but notice the worn-out leather jacket draped over his lean frame. It looked like it had seen better days, much like its owner.

Detective Wilson joined in, his gaze piercing as he leaned forward. "And Marcus, you were with him?"

Marcus, his shaved head gleaming under the harsh lights, let out an exasperated sigh. "Yeah, I was. We were just catching up, you know?"

Monique raised an eyebrow, her fingers tapping lightly on her own cup of coffee. She studied Marcus's worn leather boots, scuffed from countless walks through the streets of their neighborhood.

Detective Harper continued, "Jamal, we have eyewitnesses who claim they saw you near the scene of the crime. Care to explain that?"

Jamal's fingers twitched, the baseball cap barely concealing his nervousness. "Look, I might've been around there, but I didn't do nothin'. I didn't even see what happened."

Monique's eyes narrowed as she observed the worn edges of Jamal's cap. From his rap sheet, she knew Jamal was no angel, but this case didn't add up.

Marcus leaned forward, his frustration evident. "You guys gotta believe us. We ain't murderers. We've got no reason to kill anyone."

Detective Wilson exchanged a knowing glance with Detective Harper before rising from his chair. "Alright, we'll continue this in a moment. Don't go anywhere."

As the detectives left the room, Monique approached the two men. "Listen," she began, her voice lower, more soothing than the others. "I've seen my fair share of cases, and something about this one doesn't sit right with me. Tell me the truth, boys. What really happened that night?"

Jamal glanced at Marcus, a silent conversation passing between them. Then, with a heavy sigh, he began to recount the events of that fateful night, his words punctuated by the soft hiss of the overhead lights.

Jamal sighed and started his story. "We were just chilling at Tony's Bar, you know, sipping on some cheap beer. It was just a regular night, nothing out of the ordinary."

Monique leaned in, her curiosity piqued by the details he was about to share. "Go on."

Marcus, his voice gruff but warm, added, "We were catching up, reminiscing about old times. Nothing suspicious, I swear."

Jamal picked it up again, his fingers fidgeting with the frayed bill of his cap. "Then, we decided to head out. It was getting late, and we had to work the next day. We walked through the quiet streets, and that's when we heard it. A scream, like thunder on a clear night."

Monique's mind raced, her imagination painting a vivid picture of the darkened streets, the chill in the air, and the sudden screams of pain. She leaned on the table, urging them to continue.

"We didn't know what to do," Marcus admitted, his voice tinged with regret. "But we couldn't ignore it either. We followed the sound, and there, in a dimly lit alley, we found him."

Monique's heart sank as they described the lifeless body sprawled on the cold pavement, a haunting scene under the flickering streetlamp. She observed Jamal's trembling hands and Marcus's clenched fists, both bearing the weight of the traumatic encounter.

"We called 911 immediately," Jamal continued, his eyes welling up with unshed tears. "But by the time the cops arrived, it was too late."

As they recounted the arrival of the police, Monique couldn't help but notice the rapid twitching of Marcus's left pinkie.

"We stayed there," Marcus said, "answering questions from the officers. We thought we were helping, but now, we're here, being treated like suspects."

Monique nodded in understanding, her detective instincts telling her that there was more to this story than met the eye. She couldn't ignore the genuine fear in their voices, but she had an eerie feeling about them at the same time.

"We didn't do it," Jamal said, his voice cracking with emotion. "We're just two guys caught in the wrong place at the wrong time. There were other people there too—"

"White people!" Marcus interjected, angrily slamming his fist on the table as he looked at Monique. His eyes were searching for something in hers.

Monique knew what it was. Empathy. He had singled her out in a police station filled with white police officers and wanted to see his struggle resonate in her. Too bad she wasn't a mirror. "I'm pretty sure that they spoke to everyone on the scene."

Monique couldn't deny the complexity of their situation. The pieces of the puzzle were falling into place, but there were still missing fragments hidden beneath the surface.

The detectives returned, their faces unreadable masks of authority. Detective Wilson, his gaze still fixed on Jamal and Marcus, spoke in a measured tone. "We're going to need to verify your alibis and gather more evidence. You're not off the hook yet."

Marcus clenched his jaw, but Jamal's voice trembled with a mix of frustration and fear. "We understand, Detective. We'll cooperate in any way we can."

As the detectives left the room once more, Monique exchanged a glance with the two black youths. She could see the fear in their eyes, the nagging doubt that justice might not be on their side.

With a sigh, Monique leaned closer to them. "Listen, guys," she began, her voice softer now, "I believe you. But we need to find evidence to clear your names. Do you remember anything else from that night? Anything that might help?"

Jamal rubbed his temples, struggling to recall every detail. "There was a woman, Detective. She was there in the alley when we found the body. She seemed... strange like she knew more than she was letting on."

Monique's curiosity was piqued. "A woman? Can you describe her?"

"Yeah, for sure. She had crazy ass red hair, and her han—"

Marcus slammed his hand on the table, hitting Jamal with his boots. His eyes flashed with an unspoken warning, and Jamal went silent. "I told you to stop spouting bullshit. You're still high, man."

Monique noted Jamal's brief description carefully, her mental gears turning. A mysterious woman with fiery red hair in a dimly lit alley on the night of the murder - it was a lead, albeit a cryptic one. Marcus was starting to look suspicious, too.

"We'll look into it," Monique assured them. "But you have to promise me one thing - stay out of trouble. Don't do anything that might make you look guilty. Let us handle this."

Jamal nodded, a glimmer of hope returning to his eyes. "We will, Detective. We just want to clear our names."

Monique rose from her chair, her gaze unwavering. "I'll do everything I can to help you guys. But remember, this is just the beginning. There are twists and turns in every case, and we'll uncover them one by one."

That evening, Monique found herself back at Tony's Bar, retracing Jamal and Marcus's steps. The dimly lit establishment was a haven for regulars, its walls adorned with faded sports memorabilia and the echoes of countless stories.

Monique leaned against the worn wooden bar, sipping on a lukewarm beer. She struck up conversations with patrons, subtly probing for information about the night of the murder. It was a delicate dance of words and gestures, a skill she had honed over the years.

It was a grizzled old regular who finally broke the silence. "You're asking about that red-haired lady from the murder night, ain't ya?"

Monique's heart quickened. "Yes. Tell me everything you know."

The regular leaned in, his voice barely above a whisper. "She's trouble, that one. Always showing up when something bad's about to happen. People say she's got some kind of sixth sense, or maybe she's just a bad omen."

Monique pressed for more details, gathering snippets of information about the woman's appearances at various crime scenes, each more mysterious than the last. It was as if she had a knack for being in the wrong place at the wrong time.

As Monique left the bar, she couldn't help but wonder if this red-haired woman was the key to unraveling the case's twists and turns. But finding her would be like chasing a ghost in the night.

Monique stepped out of the soft music of the bar and into the cold night. She pulled her jacket tighter around her and walked down to the same dimly lit alley where the murder had occurred. That's when she saw her – the woman with fiery red hair. She was standing under the same flickering street lamp, her ethereal presence sending a chill down Monique's spine.

With a rush of adrenaline, Monique approached her, her voice steady but filled with urgency. "I need to talk to you."

The woman turned, her piercing green eyes locking onto Monique's. "You've been looking for me, haven't you?"

Monique nodded, her heart pounding in her chest. "I need to know what you know about that night."

"It's not what I know, Detective. It's what I can show you." The red-haired woman smiled, a cryptic, knowing smile.

With that, she turned and walked deeper into the shadows of the alley. The red-haired woman led Monique Carter through a labyrinth of dimly lit alleyways, their footsteps echoing in the silence of the night. Her heart raced as she followed this mysterious figure, her instincts telling her that she was about to uncover the final piece of the puzzle.

They reached a secluded spot, where a single streetlamp cast an eerie glow on the cracked pavement. The woman turned to Monique, her green eyes shimmering. "You're close to the truth, detective, but are you sure you want to know?"

Monique's resolve remained unshaken. "I don't care about the price. I need to know what happened that night."

The woman nodded and, with a flick of her wrist, produced a faded photograph from the folds of her flowing dress. She handed it to Monique. It was a picture of the murder victim, Seth, whose death had set this complex chain of events in motion.

Monique studied the photograph, her eyes narrowing as she noticed a distinctive tattoo on the victim's forearm – the same "Brooklyn" tattoo that Marcus had. The realization hit her like a bolt of lightning. Marcus wasn't as innocent as he portrayed himself to be.

Monique had Marcus right where she wanted him. That bloody rat.

The following morning, the police station buzzed with activity. Officers rushed around, carrying out their duties, while Jamal and Marcus remained in the same uncomfortable chairs, their anxiety palpable. Monique Carter had been up all night, piecing together the scattered clues from their story and trying to make sense of it all.

As she entered the room, Detective Harper followed closely behind. Monique wore a thoughtful expression as she regarded Marcus, whose demeanor had shifted slightly overnight. He seemed more restless, his eyes darting around the room like a cornered animal.

"Marcus," Monique began, her voice steady but probing, "I need to ask you some more questions. Can you tell me about your relationship with the victim? Have you seen him before that night? Did you have any disagreements with him?"

"Nah, Detective, I didn't even know the guy. Never seen him before that night." Marcus shifted uncomfortably in his chair, his leather jacket seeming to weigh him down.

Monique nodded slowly, filing away his response for later consideration. "And you, Jamal, did Marcus mention anything about the victim? Anything unusual? Are you sure you were with Marcus throughout last night?"

"No, Detective, we were just catching up. We didn't talk about anyone else, and we…. we were together throughout." Jamal shook his head with emphasis on each word, his eyes meeting Monique's with a mixture of determination and fear.

Detective Harper, ever observant, leaned in closer. "But Marcus, you said you followed the sound of the scream. Why? What made you want to get closer to the crime scene?"

Marcus's jaw clenched, and he glanced at Jamal as if seeking reassurance. "We, uh, wanted to see if we could help, you know if someone needed assistance."

Monique exchanged a knowing look with Detective Harper. There was something about Marcus's responses that didn't quite add up.

As they left the room, Monique decided to speak with some witnesses from that fateful night. She approached Officer Wilson, who had responded to the call and went to the scene.

"Wilson," she began, "tell me about the witnesses at the crime scene. Did anyone mention seeing Marcus or Jamal near the victim?"

Officer Wilson scratched his head, his mustache twitching as he thought. "Well, there was this one guy, a hobo, who walks the streets. He claimed he saw Marcus arguing with the victim before the gunshot. He's high half the time, so I wouldn't trust his words."

Monique raised an eyebrow. Gary's statement added a new layer of complexity to the case. She thanked Officer Wilson and headed to the nearby convenience store to speak with Gary.

Gary, a lanky man with a perpetual scowl, leaned on the wall. Monique approached, her badge displayed prominently. "Gary, I heard you saw Marcus arguing with the victim. Can you tell me more?"

Gary wiped his hands on his faded plaid shirt, his eyes darting around nervously. "Yeah, I saw 'em. He was heated and real loud like he had some kind of beef with the guy."

Monique pressed further. "Did you hear what they were arguing about?"

Gary hesitated before replying, "Well, the victim owed him some money, I think. They were shouting about it."

Monique's mind raced as she considered this new information. A debt, an argument, and now witnesses claiming to have seen Jamal and Marcus in conflict with the victim. The pieces were falling into place, and Marcus's role in this twisted puzzle was becoming increasingly suspicious.

Back at the station, she watched Marcus through the two way window of the interrogation room. Monique couldn't help but wonder if she was on the verge of unmasking the killer, hidden behind layers of deception and secrets.

As the investigation intensified, Monique Carter's suspicion of Marcus deepened, casting a long shadow over the interrogation room. Minute details and unsettling inconsistencies in his narrative had set off alarm bells, prompting her to take a more aggressive approach.

"Marcus," Monique asserted, her tone unwavering, "we've delved deeper into this case, and something just doesn't add up. It's time to discuss the events of that night with greater precision."

Marcus fidgeted in his chair, sweat forming on his brow. His gaze darted between Monique and Jamal, who had moved from concern to a volatile blend of fear and bewilderment.

Undeterred, Monique pressed forward. "You claimed you followed the sound of the gunshot to the crime scene. But why, Marcus? What compelled you to get closer?"

Marcus hesitated, his eyes dropping to the floor. "I... I wanted to check if the guy was still breathing and if there was anything we could do to help."

Leaning in, Monique locked eyes with Marcus. "Marcus, our investigation has uncovered evidence that contradicts your account. There's a surveillance camera near the alley, and it captured your movements that night. Care to clarify why the footage shows you leaving the scene rather than rendering aid?"

"And you, Jamal." She shot the shaking man a stern gaze. "Why were you nowhere in sight until the police cars started pulling up?"

Marcus stumbled over his words, his complexion turning pale. "I... I didn't even notice the camera. Maybe I was in shock."

Raising an eyebrow, Monique's skepticism hung heavily in the room. "In shock, or attempting to avoid being caught on tape?"

At that moment, Detective Wilson entered, clutching a blood-stained shirt as if unveiling a sinister secret.

"Monique, we stumbled upon something interesting at Marcus's place."

"My house? You searched my house!" Marcus exclaimed, jumping up to his feet.

Monique shifted her attention to Detective Wilson and the damning evidence. Dread rippled through her as she asked, "Marcus, care to explain why we uncovered this shirt, stained with the victim's blood, in your apartment?"

Aghast, Marcus's paled, his gaze darting frantically around the room, a desperate plea in his eyes. "I swear, I don't know how that got there. I didn't kill anyone!"

With a steely resolve, Monique leaned in, her voice a controlled whisper. "The evidence is stacking against you, Marcus. There's motive, a heated argument with the victim, and now, physical proof linking you to the crime. Tell me the truth right now!"

Jamal, sitting nearby, bore witness to the unfolding drama with a cocktail of shock and fear. "Marcus, man, you've got to come clean. You swore that you didn't do it. If you didn't do it, you need to say so now."

Tears welled in his eyes, and Marcus finally yelled. "Okay, okay, I did it! But it was an accident, I swear! That motherfucker owed me money and didn't want to pay up. I just hit him a couple of times."

A heavy silence enveloped the room as Marcus confessed to the crime. The truth, a bitter pill to swallow, had finally come to light. Monique's heart sank as the realization hit her. Marcus had been the perpetrator all along, and his desperate attempts to conceal the truth had only deepened the pit he had dug himself into.

As the confession hung in the air, Jamal stared at Marcus, his shock and sense of betrayal etched across his face. Justice had been served, but the aftermath left a bitter taste in the room, a stark reminder of the dark underbelly that could lurk beneath even the closest of friendships.

Seth, the dead guy, was actually friends with Marcus. They were in the same frat in college, and they got their first tattoos together, but this was the grisly end over a couple thousand bucks.

Monique couldn't help but reflect on the complexity of human nature and the unexpected darkness that could dwell beneath the surface, even in those one thought they knew best. Even Jamal wouldn't go unpunished. He helped in covering up a crime and providing a false alibi. The resolution had come at a heavy cost, but justice, in all its harsh reality, had been delivered.

It sure hit different when the truth is not what you expected. It hurts even more when you can't trust a friend for the truth.

CHAPTER TEN

Relationships Hit Different When You Fix Your Issues.

Chantelle sat in her cramped office, the flickering fluorescent lights overhead doing nothing to improve her mood. Her fingers danced across the keyboard, drafting yet another legal brief, while her mind wandered to the elusive partnership that seemed to slip through her fingers like water.

She had worked tirelessly for years, putting in endless hours and sacrificing time with her daughter, Alicia, to climb the ladder at the prestigious law firm of Donovan & Barnes. Yet, despite her impeccable track record and unwavering determination, the coveted partnership always eluded her grasp.

Her boss, Victor, had promised her. "Just a few months."

Chantelle had remained the very epitome of patience, but the office meeting earlier that morning had been the last straw. She had presented a compelling argument for their big case, complete with mountains of evidence, but she found herself outnumbered by her white male colleagues. They dismissed her ideas with a condescending chuckle, leaving her seething with frustration.

Her phone buzzed as she brooded over her keyboard in her office, jolting her back to reality. It was a call from

Alicia, who had just turned twenty-one. Their relationship had been strained ever since the bitter divorce from Alicia's father, John when she was just thirteen.

Chantelle answered the call, her voice strained. "Hey, Alicia."

"Mom," Alicia's voice sounded warm yet distant, a hint of apprehension hiding behind her words. "Are you coming home for dinner tonight?"

Chantelle sighed, feeling the weight of her responsibilities bearing down on her. "I wish I could, honey, but I've got another late night at the office. It's this big case, you know how it is."

Alicia's disappointment was palpable through the phone. "It's always work, Mom. You promised you'd make it home today at least."

Chantelle winced, guilt gnawing at her. "I know, Alicia, and I'm sorry. Just a little longer, okay? I promise we'll make it up this weekend. How about we catch a movie or something?"

There was a pause on the other end of the line, and Chantelle could almost hear Alicia's internal struggle. "Fine. But you owe me one."

Relief washed over Chantelle. "Deal, sweetie. I love you."

"Yeah, sure. Bye, Mom," Alicia replied, her tone softening.

Chantelle hung up and leaned back in her creaky office chair, her thoughts turning back to the infuriating meeting earlier. She couldn't shake the feeling that her colleagues were deliberately holding her back. The unfairness of it all ignited a fire within her.

With newfound determination, Chantelle returned to her keyboard, her fingers flying across the keys as she formulated a plan to prove herself in the upcoming trial. She would show her colleagues that she was not to be underestimated, and she would make partner on her own terms.

The hours passed, and the office grew dark around her as Chantelle worked tirelessly into the night. The clatter of her keyboard echoed in the empty halls until well into midnight when the continuous wave of sleep crashed over her.

She barely managed to drive home, leaning against the flower pots as she pushed open the front door, her exhaustion still clinging to her like a stubborn stain. It was a relief to finally be away from the oppressive atmosphere at work, but as her eyes darted around the living room, something felt amiss.

Alicia was a night owl, just like her father, too much like her father. Chantelle would rather die than admit it, but Alicia reminded her too much of John, the man who tried but failed to clip her wings. She couldn't make Alicia hate him, but she felt betrayed on those weekends spent alone while John spent time with her daughter.

"Alicia?" Chantelle called out, hoping but knowing full well that Alicia wasn't home. Alicia loved parties and ensured she attended every single one. A free spirit in every sense of the word, probably why Chantelle couldn't discourage her from taking two gap years after high school.

She groaned, kicking off her heels as she headed towards her daughter's room, which she had rarely

visited in the past eight years. She was too busy, too late, too engrossed in files ahead of a hearing.
Too absent.
As she pushed the door open, her heart skipped a beat. The room that had once been the center of their morning rituals and bedtime stories when Alicia was younger now felt like a foreign land. Alicia's bed was neatly made, a UCLA Jersey carelessly strewn on top of it.
"Alicia," Chantelle sighed, her eyes fixed on the empty room and the stacked luggage in the corner. The realization struck her like a punch to the gut. Alicia was going off to college the next day. She had promised to make a goodbye dinner, and Chantelle had agreed to it, albeit absentmindedly.
She hadn't been here for Alicia in a long time. No more waking her up with a gentle nudge, no more calls for breakfast before school. Her baby had grown up, and she had been absent for it all.
Tears welled in her eyes as she moved further into the room, her fingers grazing the walls covered in Alicia's artwork. They were no longer the colorful, playful drawings that used to find a home on their refrigerator. Instead, they were a dark and haunting testament to her daughter's transition into adulthood.
Dark, distorted lines ran from each side of the canvas to the other. She ran her hand over one particular piece, the rough sensation sending shivers down her spine. It was the silhouette of a girl, her face obscured by shadows, standing on the edge of a cliff. Deep blues and stark blacks created an eerie, almost otherworldly atmosphere.

Chantelle blinked back tears, the weight of her absence heavy on her shoulders. "I missed so much, didn't I?" Alicia's room offered no answers, silent and unresponsive. Her daughter's journey from childhood innocence to the complex emotions of adulthood had unfolded within these four walls, and Chantelle had been too consumed by her career to notice.

Even the career had been nothing but a disappointment, taking all her time and leaving her with nothing but disappointments and regrets.

With a heavy heart, Chantelle sank onto Alicia's bed, clutching the UCLA Jersey as if it were a lifeline. She couldn't turn back time, but she could make a change. It was time to be there for her daughter, to bridge the gap that had formed between them.

As she sat there in the stillness of the room, her eyes landed on a blue journal, splayed open with a pen next to it. Alicia probably forgot to close it. A quote written in blue ink caught her attention.

Beauty is no quality in things themselves. It exists merely in the mind which contemplates them.
- David Hume.

Chantelle knew in this moment that she had somehow made her daughter perceive the world through dark lenses. "I'll fix this… I'll fix us." She made a silent promise to herself. She would find a way to connect with Alicia, to understand the person she had become. And maybe, just maybe, she could help her daughter navigate the darkness that now filled her artwork.

The next day, Chantelle's heart started beating fast the next day as she descended the stairs. Her beach bag slammed against her hips as she walked, and her long black hair stuck to her sweaty neck. She scanned the beach, trying to locate her brown skinned bombshell of a daughter.

The expectation was to find her in a large group of rowdy frat boys, but she was alone, standing in a pair of blue shorts and a red flannel shirt.

"Alicia!" Chantelle hollered, ignoring the curious looks of dog walkers and random beachgoers.

"Mom, how did you find me!" Alicia exclaimed, her blue eyes wide with surprise.

"A little birdie whispered it to me," Chantelle replied, flashing her an infectious smile.

Alicia never changed, from her pitch black hair to her blue eyes inherited from her white dad. Even her height, she had always towered over all the other kids in school, so it was a no brainer when she joined the basketball team in high school.

Fitting right in and standing out at the same time.

Chantelle had spent the whole day stalking her daughter on TikTok and Instagram. Finding her location at Gunnison Beach was easier than she thought it would be. The tags and comments from last night's wild party were easy to notice only when you knew where to find them. "Where are all your friends from the party last night?"

"I don't know, at home, maybe?" Alicia shrugged, still frowning in confusion and surprise.

Chantelle took in deep breaths, feeling her sundress swaying around her ankles. "I'm not here to pick a fight with you. Come on, let's set up the perfect spot."

"What?"

"I'm trying to be nice. Stop testing me with your endless questions."

"Damn. Okay, okay." Alicia hurried after her and grabbed the corner of a blanket that Chantelle dug out from her knit bag.

They spread the blanket, and Alicia uncorked the wine that her mother had brought. Chantelle looked at her, hunched over, and couldn't help but feel a warm glow of pride. "You know I'm proud of you, right."

Alice's fingers paused over the bottle, and she looked at her in further confusion, uncomfortable with the sudden words of affirmation. "Okay. You know I'm not yet twenty one, right?"

"What?" Chantelle chuckled, realizing that she was now the one with the dumb questions.

"The wine. Technically, I'm underage, and you're a lawyer."

The sudden urge to be the cool parent while still sticking to the law made Chantelle subconsciously raise her shoulders. "It is illegal for younglings like you under the age of twenty one to drink buttttt...," she drew out the final letter, "it's legal only and only if it's coming from your parents or your guardian."

"You really know how to make a girl feel special," Alicia grinned, leaning back and raising her glass in a toast.

Chantelle chuckled, eyes locked onto her daughter. "Well, you deserve it. Things have been messy recently, and I've not been there for you as much as I should. I just want to see you happy again."

"I'm happy." Alice offered a weary smile, pouring wine into her glass.

Chantelle felt a lump forming in her throat, her eyes stinging with unshed tears. "You're not. I know you're not."

"Pray tell mum, how did you find out?"

Silence descended between them as they sipped on the wine until the bottle turned clear. The sun dipped below the horizon, painting the sky in hues of orange and pink. And the empty bottle of wine rolled down into the water.

Alicia leaned her head onto Chantelle's lap, her mind wandering again. "It's so beautiful," she whispered.

Chantelle's eyes softened as she stroked the dark curls she used to braid, "Not as beautiful as you."

"You're just saying that to make me feel better. I'm like a white wall in a colorful room. The best I can do is oddly stand out. Nothing more."

"That's not true, Alicia. You're beautiful, you're athletic, you're smart, and you're amazing." Chantelle could feel her heartbreak with every word of reassurance that was obviously coming too late.

All the chances she had to whisper those words seemed to have slipped through her fingers like fine sand.

Tears welled up in Chantelle's eyes as Alicia looked up at her. "You know, I never thought this day would come so fast. I know I complained about your gap years, but a part of me felt grateful."

"What? You scolded and shouted all day; that was the most I'd ever heard from you at once in years," Alicia exclaimed, trying to control the corners of her lips that were tugging up into a smile.

Chantelle winced at the slight barb hidden in Alicia's words. "It all came from a place of love and worry. You were acting weird at that point, and you never talked to me about your decision. I had to hear about it from your dad and…"

She hated it. She had custody of Alicia throughout the moments when she made those decisions, but still, she had to hear about it from John. It sparked a fuse that led to a loud argument in the kitchen. Milk was spilled, pancakes stained the floors, and voices filled the air. It was unpleasant, to say the least.

"I'm sorry. I should have spoken to you before making my final decision," Alicia admitted. "I guess a part of me also wanted to spite you. You threw yourself into your work after the divorce and abandoned me. I lost my parents, too. You guys just became Mom and Dad. Thirteen year old me definitely didn't comprehend immediately."

Chantelle gently wiped away Alicia's tears with her thumb. "I am sorry, Alicia. For my absence, for my ignorance, for everything. I am sorry. None of it was your fault, and blaming you was wrong."

Alicia took a deep breath, trying to steady her emotions. "You're being sappy; stop it."

"No, you're my baby, and you're leaving tomorrow. I get to be sappy all I want." Chantelle felt her belly cramp up from her laughter as she hugged Alicia tightly. "I think I'm the happiest mom alive right now," she said, her voice filled with joy.

"It's fine to be happy. I like it when you're happy." Alicia rolled onto her side, burying her face into Chantelle's belly.

Chantelle could feel the vibrations from her belly as she spoke. "I like it when you're happy too. It makes me very happy."

The night seemed to pass by too fast as Chantelle and Alicia shared funny and heartwarming conversations. They laughed and talked about their plans for the future, trash talking Chantelle's boss for a solid minute until all the animosity was out of their systems.

The sky gradually turned from inky black to a faint shade of blue, indicating the beginning of a new day. Alicia reluctantly suggested they head back home. The beach was almost empty now, save for a few early risers. They got up, brushing the sand off their clothes. Alicia hesitated momentarily and held the half folded blanket in mid air. "Hey, Mom, do you mind if I drive us home?" she asked with excitement in her eyes.

Chantelle blinked in surprise. Alicia had learned how to drive from her dad, but Chantelle had never allowed her to drive her car. She gazed at her daughter for a moment, then surprised her by tossing the car keys to her.

Alicia caught the keys, her eyes wide with disbelief. "Seriously, Mom?"

Chantelle smiled, feeling a sense of trust she hadn't felt in years. "Seriously. Go ahead, show me what you've got."

With an excited grin, Alicia skipped to the car and got behind the wheel, tapping excitedly as Chantelle settled into the passenger seat. They both fastened their seatbelts with a sense of anticipation. As Alicia started the engine, the car roared to life, and they pulled away from the beach, leaving behind the memories of that magical night.

The short drive home felt like an adventure for Alicia. She handled the car with confidence and enthusiasm, making Chantelle proud. As they settled back into the house, Alicia looked at her half-packed luggage with a sigh. "I still have so much to pack, Mom."

Chantelle, feeling grateful for the opportunity to be involved in her daughter's life again, offered to help. "I could help out if you want me to, of course."
"I would love it if you could."
They worked together until sunrise, folding clothes and packing toiletries. It was a bittersweet moment as they packed away the memories of Alicia's childhood, but Chantelle couldn't be happier.
After they had finished packing, they collapsed onto Alicia's bed, exhausted but content. Their laughter filled the room as they made plans for Alicia's college journey.

~~~~~~~~~

A week had passed the night on the beach, and Chantelle found herself alone at the kitchen counter. The aroma of freshly brewed coffee wafted through the air, filling the room with its comforting warmth as she took a sip, relishing the rich taste.
With a sense of pride, she reached into her pocket and retrieved a golden partner badge. It had been a long and arduous journey to earn that coveted title at the law firm, and now, it gleamed proudly on her suit jacket. She carefully pinned it in place, the metal clinking softly against the fabric.
Her gaze drifted to the wall beside the refrigerator, where a new addition had popped up a week ago. It was a large, breathtaking painting of a sunrise. The colors blended together in a display of oranges, pinks, and purples, casting a warm and inviting glow throughout the kitchen. Right at the bottom left corner, a name was elegantly signed—Alicia.

Alicia's voice from their call last night echoed in her mind as she admired the artwork. "Mom, you deserve that badge. You've worked so hard for it."

Chantelle sighed contentedly, grateful for the renewed connection with her daughter. She knew that being a partner at the law firm was a significant achievement, but it paled in comparison to the joy of mending their fractured relationship.

Just then, her phone buzzed with a message notification, and she picked it up to see a text from Alicia. "Hey, Mom! Just wanted to remind you I love you."

Tears welled up in Chantelle's eyes as she replied, "I love you too, Alicia. You mean the world to me. Can't wait to see you again."

With a contented heart and the painting of the sunrise as a constant reminder of their renewed bond, Chantelle returned to her coffee, feeling a sense of fulfillment that surpassed any professional achievement.

It hits different when you mend broken relationships.

Epilogue

So, we've rolled through the crazy stories of "Hit Different" – where life took a detour, threw some crazy curveballs, and had us all feeling some type of way. It's been one wild ride, and here we are, picking up the pieces and making sense of it all.

Life in a world post covid where Black Twitter is a thing ain't ever straightforward, that's for sure. It's like trying to navigate a maze with no map, and just when you think you've got the hang of it, bam! Plot twist! That's what makes these tales in "Hit Different" so damn engaging and relatable.

These stories are not 100% fiction and I am sure you know somebody or you yourself have experienced something closely similar. We all know the dream-chasers, hustlers, and survivors. They faced or face their battles head-on, and just when they thought they were in control, life laughed and showed 'em who's boss.

But here's the scoop, fam. Life ain't always about the punches it throws. It's about how you bob and weave and roll with the punches, how you adapt and come back stronger. These characters in "Hit Different" proved that there is still life on the other side of the hit.

So, as we close this book, remember this – life's gonna hit you different, but that's where the real magic happens. It's in those twists, those unexpected turns, and those moments when you're feeling a way that you find your true self. Keep riding the wave, keep hitting different, and keep living life on your terms.

Thanks for vibing with us and experiencing our stories. Thanks for being a part of "Hit Different." Until next time, keep it real and stay woke!

Thanks For Reading

I would love to hear what you thought of the book, Please leave me a review. Tell me which story was your favorite. If I can get enough votes for a story I will write a whole book on those characters.